Nyifie Brothers Publishing

THE ISLAND

JOHNNY B. TRUANT

SEAN PLATT

THE ISLAND

Chapter One

AT THE FAR end of the island, near what became a fuel depot, was a long and unruly dock whose origin Gerd could not recall. Atticus claimed not to remember it either, but the thing was poorly considered to the point of whimsy, seemingly created by lazy focus and refusal to obey the way physics and fluid dynamics were supposed to work. And that, right there, was Atticus to a T.

Who needs laws? Who needs science?

Atticus was above such things. There were rules, and there were implications, and whereas Gerd tended to treat the latter as if they were the former, Atticus never had. His disrespect courted anarchy. But while Atticus could have lived quite happily in chaos, that had never been Gerd's style.

Gerd looked at the dock, hating the way it tainted the otherwise pristine shore. His own dock was gone. Forgotten. It was either this dock or make a new one. He scoffed. Atticus said he didn't remember creating the dock? Well, it hadn't come from Gerd.

He walked to the end, annoyed by the way the thing

floated without pylons, the entire structure swishing in the boundless ocean like the island wagging its tail. The boards creaked. The paint flecks (red; that was fitting) came off on his hands as he held the rails.

Upon reaching the end, Gerd knelt as he did every time, cursing the dock as he did every time. Then he took the rope and began to hoist it … as he did, every time.

Soon after beginning, though, he stopped. His attention had been caught by a seashell on the dock. Just one, but it was postcard perfect and Gerd found himself transfixed. Who'd put it there? Atticus? It didn't seem like Atticus-type whimsy.

Hey there, shell. Shel, he found himself thinking at it. And then something almost-remembered,

(would you like to play a game?)

before it was gone like everything else. Gerd found himself somehow lost even with the line in his hands, as if he'd never been here before.

He's playing with you, Gerd told himself. *The asshole* always *plays with you. Don't let him win, Gerd. Don't let him rock your boat, with his convenient little lies.*

It was enough to break the spell. Gerd was immediately himself again, and when he thought to look back at where the shell *(Shel)* had been, he found that it was no longer there. Kicked into the deep blue nothing while he'd been rooting around, probably. But why did he even care?

Gerd shook his head. The air was hot and the sky was clear, and he had things to do. Stay near the water too long and the shark always came. He could see its enormous dorsal fin, circling thirty feet from the dock's end, just daring Gerd to do more than what he'd come here to do.

"Just stay there," Gerd said, as if the shark could hear him.

Raising the cage took ten minutes. The shark, mollified

by proper duty, kept its distance. On the dock behind Gerd, the rope made a pile that rose overhead. In the past, he'd looped the impossibly long thing around the posts, but these days it was easier to pile. It wasn't like it'd stay that way. The mistake wasn't really forgetting. It was in forgetting how impossible it sometimes could be to truly remember.

There was a lobster cage with three rocks inside at the end of the rope.

The stones were obsidian black.

Gerd sighed.

And muttered aloud, "Of course."

SIX MILES north by a conventional compass, Gerd put his pickup in park. The vehicle had come to him dust-covered, spattered with mud like some kind of joke. The interior smelled like gravy. Magazines, mail, and opened containers that had once housed everything from electronic components to fast food filled the cabin, mostly settled in the passenger-side footwell. He'd cleaned them out before, but didn't bother anymore. No matter what he did, they always came back.

He got out, tossing his excavation bag onto the ground, and slammed the door. Then he stared at the old truck for a long while, but of course nothing happened.

Sighing, Gerd hiked the bag over one shoulder. It weighed approximately a billion pounds. He'd probably be crippled for hours afterward. He might have to make threats to feel well again.

He stood straight, acknowledging the weight. After long seconds, he'd accepted it enough to move. Things were always easier after the initial shock. But oh boy would he make Atticus pay for this later.

Legs trudging forward, Gerd reached the pit. He dropped the bag with a clang, then reached inside. He'd been given an L-1. A Persuader. And of course plenty of decoys.

He'd made two traps, and with his back already aching, he took the smaller one from his bag.

Gerd descended two steps into the pit — low enough that his feet disturbed a delicate rock scree and the sky started to darken — before he swore and turned suddenly back.

Three. Motherfucker. There'd been *three* stones in the lobster cage.

The small trap held only two Unwanted. So of course he'd have to lug the big one.

BELOW THE PIT'S upper lip but before the hellscape appeared, Gerd encountered a ten-foot bad idea half-materialized and more or less sitting on a rock.

"Password?" it said.

Gerd tried not to look directly at the thing, like Atticus wanted him to. Peripheral vision was enough for function, showing him skin as red as the dock had once been and horns the size of elephant tusks.

"Fuck your mother," Gerd told it.

"That's not the password."

Gerd waited, still looking at it sidelong.

"That's not the password," the thing repeated.

"Are you blocking my way?"

Calling its bluff. He'd learned that particular trick several thousand years ago, and yet Atticus still saw this as funny.

"You shall not pass."

"Yeah, yeah." Gerd flapped a hand and walked by the

sentinel, daring it to pursue him but knowing it never would. That kind of thing required too much energy. Too many of what Atticus jokingly called hit points.

Gerd entered the lower level, still with that newly blighted sky above the pit — so much less welcoming than the island sky theoretically still up there somewhere. He stayed to the side, feet navigating a carved-in edge that was barely substantial enough to hold his weight. The air smelled like sulfur. Gerd, thanks to the skin glands he'd never learned to disavow, was immediately sweating like a pig.

The shaft mine lay ahead, its entrance a rock-hewn rectangle at the pit's near-bottom. Everything here was red, scarlet, crimson. The soundscape was all screaming and grunts. Gerd barely heard it anymore.

He waited at the entrance until a sound like rice poured slowly onto a hard tile floor rippled toward him. It was too dark to see everything inside the shaft's mouth, but Gerd sensed movement. He waited for his eyes to adjust but the Gatekeeper had assembled itself before they did, so he could only vaguely see it — thousands of arachnids and beetles that could only speak once all those bugs had piled into a single being.

"You," it said as roaches spilled from its lips.

"Me."

"Do you come with demands?"

"Yes. Three." Gerd opened a small drawstring bag and showed the Gatekeeper the stones he'd pulled from the water.

"Which three of the Unwanted will you take?"

"Any that fulfill the stones."

"You take their fates into your hands." The Gatekeeper seemed to chuckle. Then, after Gerd said nothing, waiting for more, the Gatekeeper finally sighed and said, "Fine. Go on in."

THE CABIN WAS DIFFERENT. Again.

In Gerd's absence, Atticus had added a new wing, no doubt filled with tasteful Renaissance nudes. But despite its sense of promised art, the new wing was garish. The shore was all tall weeds and tangles, and beyond the seafront deck were rocks and a wooden walkway rising above them, then beyond that a beach that quite literally went on forever if anyone wanted it to.

A perfect beach house location, not a plot for a bastardized McMansion. Everything felt less tranquil with his prison like this — as if the cabin's mere presence was somehow a robust shout over nature's song.

Gerd was too ichor-covered and exhausted from killing creatures to deal with it now.

Add a wing. Destroy a wing. Add a wing again. Destroy it again.

The cycle was juvenile and tiresome, like two children quarreling over the last cookie.

The quaint wooden front door had become a fortress gate. Gerd had to lean his weight outward against the handle to budge the thing — enough that for a small while, he thought that Atticus had finally found a way to seal him out.

But that was absurd. He was just tired. From the heavy bag, the shitty truck, and the three damn stones.

The door opened with a squeal. Gerd controlled the foyer, so it wasn't offensive. The space was small and modest: a coat stand, wood paneling, a plastic tray for soiled shoes. The discord of design alone should have stopped all the bickering.

He'd left the weapons and the rest of his excavation

equipment in the truck, but the trap itself had grown heavy with three Unwanted inside. He'd pulled out the guns and put the trap in the bag to drag it, across the half-sand lawn and over the threshold. Looking back once inside, he saw that its weight had cut a pair of deep ruts through the sandstone tile. Oh well. The ruts would be gone by morning.

The fortress door had shut on its own. After all the evening sounds outside, the cabin's foyer was still. Gerd let go of the bag, deciding to drag it into the basement later.

He stood straight. Then there was a sharp pain in the center of his chest and a sense of pressure that seemed to start small and push outward from the center.

He looked down to see the tip of a sword, half covered in blood. He'd been run through with a blade, his heart punctured and spilling its life onto the floor.

"Welcome home," said Atticus behind him.

Chapter Two

A LONG TIME AGO, in a land far away, a prince and princess lived in a large and awe-inspiring castle.

The stronghold stood on sprawling grounds of lush grass, dappled with pear trees that were always in season. Long pastures lined with white fences crawled from hill to hill, where the most beautiful horses grazed. It was a lovely life, and in it, the prince and princess were happy.

The princess was clever, smart, and lovely. A genius with those she served, always able to create harmony between those inclined to disagree. She brokered fair deals and kept the people's records in pristine order.

Most of all, the princess was kind. To be around her was like basking in the light of a warm day. The princess lifted spirits and healed the sick. She shunned the darkness whenever it came.

The prince was talented and creative, spending his days smithing words when not wrist-deep in paints and clay. He told the most wonderful, most fanciful stories, to entertain the people. His portraits were so real, they would have passed, in our world, for photographs.

Together they were perfect.

And so it was until one day, a stranger arrived.

Chapter Three

Dinner was quiet, save the clinking of silverware against plates, and the muted thunk of wineglasses being picked up and set back down. Atticus had decorated the dining room like a gothic cathedral: all saints meeting their deaths depicted in stained glass on windows that were, strictly speaking, too large for the cabin's actual size. A chandelier hung overhead, crowded with lit candles. Atticus hadn't known to use catch saucers, so the tallow sconces were always dripping hot wax onto the nightly meat.

The table was fifteen feet long. Atticus, dressed in black, sat at one end while Gerd, still in his blood-soaked T-shirt and jeans, sat at the other. His nicked lung was mostly whole again, but it still hurt a little to breathe.

"I suppose you think that was funny today," said Gerd. "With the weight of my bag."

Atticus chewed. "I thought you might need a lodestone."

Gerd waited, not wanting to dignify this with a response.

"Fine," Atticus admitted. "I thought it was funny."

"And the observatory over your wing?"

"Proof of my excellent taste."

Gerd took a bite. The meat tasted like steak, but the island had no cows. They'd never had to forage — food was the only thing the pit provided, beyond the Unwanted. Gerd had tried to branch out several times. Atticus even let him dig a garden; his adversary was nothing if not curious. But no matter what he planted, only body parts grew: fingers, lips, once something squishy and maggot-eaten that resembled a large intestine.

"It clashes," Gerd retorted.

"Clashes with what?"

"With the rest of the original cabin. And nature."

Atticus scoffed. His face was half bulging eyes. He was stick-thin: a scarecrow that'd been propped upright and taught aristocracy.

"*Nature.* Are you afraid we'll upset the fragile balance?"

"No, I'm saying your constant construction is tasteless. And I do not wish to live in poor taste."

"I see. And this is to impress all our visitors?"

"It's for myself. The appeal of this place is its simplicity. Its *lack* of grandeur, not its abundance."

"So let me get this straight: we can create whatever we want ... except nice things?" Atticus looked at him askance.

"We can't really create *whatever* we want, can we? Not unless we agree. And your opinion of what constitutes 'nice things' is very different from mine." Gerd cut more meat, curious in the ensuing beat of silence just what he was actually cutting. Usually when such thoughts struck him, it was more pleasant not to ask.

"That's because you *have* no decent opinion," Atticus said.

"And you may act on that belief all you wish in spaces I

can't touch. Do whatever you want with your wing, but don't intrude on mine." Then he added under his breath, "*Like always.*"

"I'm sorry." Atticus cupped a hand behind one ear. "What was that?"

"Never mind."

"No, Gerd. I think you have something to say."

"What's the point? It's not like you'll listen. Every time I leave, you add something to the exterior that can be seen from space."

"And?"

"And structures like that *intrude*. I can't *not see* your monstrosities. But there's nothing new here. How many times have I said it? The only real control — the only way in which we're truly free — comes from denial. From restraint. Don't you understand? Material things come out of desire, and desire causes suffering."

"I'm not suffering," Atticus told him. "I can have whatever I want."

"And that's not ironic to you?"

"What's not?"

"Greed."

"Why is that ironic? Please. Enlighten me."

So futile. He shook his head. "Never mind."

"*Never mind?* You've said that once already tonight, Gerdamene."

Head down. Eating. "Then I'm saying it again."

A moment. Then Atticus said, almost to himself, "So superior. So holier-than-thee."

"I'm sorry." Gerd cupped a hand behind his ear in mockery. "What was that?"

Atticus stood.

Gerd glanced up. "Oh, sit down."

"I still think you have something to say, and it's not

about parapets or tapestries or new additions to my wing. You are not powerless. If you want more separation, add a breezeway."

"Sit down, or I'll impale you."

"You can do whatever you want with your half. Extend it out over the water, if you love nature so much. Far enough that you can't even *see* my 'poor taste.'"

"Believe me," Gerd said, still seated and chewing. "I've tried."

"Look at me, Gerd. Damn you."

He focused on his plate while Atticus advanced.

"Gerd …"

Gerd spun around, reached behind his chair, grabbed one of Atticus's ornamental spears, then threw it hard enough to pass right through him — this time at the throat.

Atticus sputtered, coughing blood, unable to speak with an inch-thick spine through his larynx. Gore had shot through the exit wound to spatter a painting of Henry the Eighth on the chest, as if he too was a sloppy eater. Atticus seemed to have lost his motor control, meaning the spear tip had probably worked under the ridge of his skull on its way out and slashed his cerebellum. Or maybe it was just hard to maneuver with a spear through your neck. Gerd had hoped to pin him against the wall, but he hadn't used enough force and now there'd be blood everywhere.

He took two final shambling steps, the spear's long haft wagging at Gerd like a naughty finger. Then the rest of Atticus gave out and he fell onto the pole, dead.

The spear's trailing end wedged under a heavy oriental rug, propping upright like a tent pole, his body forming the lean-to.

Returning to his seat, Gerd cut more meat from the bone, wiping his lips and sipping his wine.

"Asshole," he told the corpse.

THEY AVOIDED each other after that.

Gerd retired to his wing, and after a while he heard stirring and knew that Atticus had retired to his room. There'd been much audible chaos beforehand. The spear's handle was too thick to break, so judging by the sound, Atticus had either spent enough capital to summon a saw or had made a rather awkward trip to the toolshed for the one they already had.

Hearing it all, Gerd was glad he'd taken his turn today. Atticus might behave, knowing a day of Gerd-decisions stood between now and his next shot at revenge.

He read for a while indoors, then decided to take in the evening sky. The stars were unfathomably clear.

But at the deck — in the home's center where they shared dominion — Gerd discovered that every one of the boards had been rotted, with alligators in a wallow below the joists. Piles of manure had been poured at both forward corners, obstructing the vista while turning it rank. Only one small corner remained solid, on Gerd's side of the divide.

"The beach," he said aloud.

So he walked to it. And there he found the shark: the huge, monstrous beastie that reared from the water every-where but the dock. Gerd had never even once considered heading away from the island to take a swim without the shark showing its fin or more.

The shark was fearless, and would beach itself if Gerd so much as approached the water's edge. It slid right up to him on wet sand and opened its mouth wide to hundreds of pointed teeth. Its tiny black eyes were pools of ink that seemed to follow him. And the eyes seemed to say, *Wherever you go, I go.*

"Oh, come on. It stinks up there. I just want to dip my toes."

The shark shut its huge mouth, then opened it again, the motion like licking its lips.

"Fine." So he returned to the deck and sat in the corner, trying to ignore the odor and the ruined view. The alligators kept snapping their jaws.

After a while, annoyed, Gerd went back inside, where a new cloying odor — cheap cologne — percolated from the other wing.

Atticus was going to get *so many lodestones* in his pack tomorrow.

Chapter Four

The stranger was new to the land.

He arrived on an oxen cart with trickery up his sleeves, though at first nobody knew it.

He met the prince, and the two became fast friends. They had so much in common. The stranger complimented the prince's art and read his work and encouraged him to tell more and deeper stories — the sort that reached to the bottom of the lessons the prince had to give.

But the prince did not know that the stranger brought dark magic. His words were born to flatter him, and the prince, being only a man, grew fond of this adulation. The stranger brought introductions to the right people. He brought an instrument that would take the prince's words and send them far and wide.

And so the stranger flourished one hand to bewitch the prince, while his other hand worked elsewhere.

The stranger met the princess second, though the prince did not know when he met her. As the stranger had flattered the prince, so did he flatter the princess, his every compliment carrying a sharp second edge.

And in this way, the stranger performed verbal dark magic to enchant his way with the princess.

He would tell the princess that it was okay that a third and fourth party weren't happy, because the extreme joy of the first and second was so complete.

Nobody could have satisfied everyone, he told her:

You did the very best you could, and it is excellent.

Chapter Five

"I suppose you have a full day planned," Atticus said, happening upon Gerd in the kitchen. "Breaking my back. Filling my car with garlic."

Gerd was sipping coffee. Thankfully, the drink was something Atticus also enjoyed, so they created plenty. He wished Atticus also liked toast, though for food it probably wouldn't have mattered. Breakfast was always mystery meat — rare, no matter how long it cooked.

"Your car already smells like garlic."

"An unreasonable number of demand stones, then. Will you give me five? Six? How much sway do you have over the line in the water, do you think?"

"Are you trying to give me ideas?" Gerd asked.

The coffee tasted a little like blood. That happened when Atticus was on the verge of something. It struck Gerd as a form of metastasis, or a kind of psychic menstruation.

"I don't like surprises," Atticus told him. "Whatever you have in mind, just tell me."

"I have determined a way to dismember you in your sleep," said Gerd.

Atticus laughed as if to say, *How pedestrian.*

"Without killing you."

Atticus stopped laughing. "I'm serious."

Gerd set down his coffee cup: a twelve-ounce ceramic mug that read, *DON'T TALK TO ME UNTIL I'VE HAD MY ADRENOCHROME.* He didn't know what it meant; like everything in the cabin it'd simply appeared one day. "I'm serious, too. Or perhaps I'm not."

Atticus stared him in the face. They were in a blood-spilling standoff when they heard the distant sound of falling trees: the island's warning that the day's duties refused to wait. He looked back at the door, then at Gerd with clear regret.

It seemed Atticus might tempt fate and stay to fight, but instead he paced backward toward the foyer. "We're not through talking about this," he said, rushing out.

Gerd heard his car's familiar roaring start. Atticus's vehicle was a 1976 Firebird with front clips from the '77 model added, but with two round headlamps instead of the '77's four rectangular ones. Given the specs, it had to be the same exact car from *Smokey and the Bandit*, except that Gerd had filled it with so much shit over the years that the interior had rotted to floorpan and seat springs. Neither of their vehicles ran on gasoline, but the Firebird sounded like it did — and high octane, too. For some infuriating reason they both had to refuel at the depot regardless of what their vehicles burned or sooner or later they wouldn't go anywhere.

Gerd finished his coffee, procrastinating. The blood taste was stronger at the bottom, as if he'd sipped off all the java and left only concentrate behind. The taste wasn't bad, though in a reasonable world it absolutely should have been. The contrast was confusing: Gerd liked the metallic sensation in his mouth, but loathed his enjoyment.

He poured another cup just to be sure … and yes, it still tasted of red. All this tainted liquid felt like a terrible omen. He'd wanted to ask Atticus what he was up to, but time here had a certain elasticity. Chances were, Atticus didn't *know* what he was up to yet. The blood was probably running ahead of him. So whatever kept causing it might happen this afternoon. Mentioning it to Atticus now (especially considering that Atticus, running off in a huff, hadn't poured himself a cup to know it was there) would only be giving him ideas.

Gerd sat, then turned his thoughts to Atticus's daily errand, which he was responsible for today as the one at home. It took tremendous effort to summon stones, but he found himself able to do so by picturing the dock and hating it with all his might. Once there in his mind, he deposited four, perhaps five obsidian stones into the lobster cage at the bottom of the sea.

Then he focused his mind again and put two lode-stones into Atticus's pack, while at the same time choosing him a temperamental weapon that might, if Gerd was lucky, blow his face off. If that happened, Gerd would have to cash in those stones since Atticus would be in no condition, but the effort would be worth it.

There was no way to lose.

This done, Gerd procrastinated a while longer by wandering the cabin. He paced the shared center, then his wing, and then the boundary, through which he peeked into Atticus's space and saw only tacky casino decor.

He turned to leave, then turned back. Wondering.

After summoning all those rocks for the lobster cage, did he still have capital enough with the Authority to push himself through the boundary and see Atticus's rooms up close? Probably not. Almost *certainly* not, considering that preserved separate spaces were the one thing here immutable as gravity and red meat.

Still, he kept thinking of Atticus's unusual trepidation this morning — the way that, instead of coming out swinging, he'd gone artificially cocky and practically begged Gerd to reveal his next torture. That plus the soured coffee gave Gerd chills that came on stronger than the pain. He'd learned to trust his instincts, and couldn't get to all the work he didn't want to do with this foreboding haunting the infinite hallways in his mind.

He concentrated, sent his mind upward, then walked forward into the boundary. There was a stretching sensation like pushing into plastic wrap. The invisible border flexed several inches, but then refused to stretch any more.

Damn. The sense that Atticus was up to something they'd both regret was gaining strength by the minute.

Unable to enter the inner sanctum, Gerd circled the building. He paced and stood on tiptoes, trying to see through the windows. Atticus had added a bunch of Frank Lloyd Wright in today's early hours, but the glass was mirrored and polarized — enough to blind passing ships if there ever were any.

He climbed the facade. Circled the towers. Hammered on unbreakable glass. And saw nothing.

"It's just nerves," he told himself while mounting the breakwater.

The wind swept across the sea, raising his hair. Invisible salt stuck to individual strands, making the mess feel like wadded glue when Gerd tried to smooth it with his palm.

Thunderheads were coming.

No. He didn't believe it was "just nerves" at all.

. . .

ALTHOUGH IT MADE NO DIFFERENCE, Gerd chose to keep the vault door open.

Thunderheads fought with blinding light for sky space, filling the home with solid-looking sunbeams. Now some of that abundant sunlight spilled down the basement stairs, mirroring mote-strewn secondary beams that twisted themselves even to the depths, where Gerd was working.

His labor usually came while Atticus was taking his turn at the pit. Alone in the cabin, Gerd could *always* leave the door open, if paranoia didn't keep ordering him to do otherwise. He wasn't afraid of the Unwanted finding the open door; they were his own things, and at the start the hatchlings were always helpless and small.

No, it was *Atticus's* intrusion that concerned him. Atticus might finish early; Atticus (though this was unfathomable) might blow off his turn and come back with empty hands. What if he walked right in? Nobody wanted to be seen with their Unwanted in plain sight.

Gerd unzipped the incubation tent. The three nut-sized things he'd dug from the chests of slain pit creatures yesterday were now eggs, each about the girth of an oblong softball. He checked their temperatures and found them cold enough to freeze warm breath on contact. Their green, leathery surfaces were already oozing. There were no *good* signs — no truly *good* work with the Unwanted. But it was at least a *facile* sign. One that said, *This will be finished sooner rather than later.*

If he was very lucky, they'd hatch in the next half hour or so. After dispatching them, Gerd might even have time to destroy some of the common-area eyesores Atticus had built (like this morning's topiary) and reconstruct the deck. Get a little outdoor reading in, pretending he was just a guy enjoying the beach.

One of the pods shook. Gerd poked the Unwanted,

recoiling before it could frostbite him. A branch snapped outside and he flinched hard, knocking the thing into the debris still remaining from his prior round of hatchlings. Gerd had long ago stopped cleaning away their coverings and corpses, content to know that all garbage was contained by the tent and did not smell.

Every new round of skins faded within a week anyway, same as all memories eventually did. Without Gerd's attention, none of them could exist for long. But that was true of the pain he felt when Atticus tortured him as well — or the exertion of his turns, or the condition of their vehicles, or that infernal ocean dock.

You couldn't always help what you saw or believed. Some truths were flexible. Others were as indelible as your face in the mirror, and in those cases it took superhuman amounts of denial to let them go.

Stop it. Your nerves are besting you.

Gerd righted the pod, then watched it closely. He kept his eyes on all of them (and his ears on the outside world), but still Gerd found himself staring so intently at the pod that he thought his vision might be shaking.

Was he imagining things, or was it actually hatching? And why did it matter, other than his usual desire to get this over with? He was a vulture overhead, neck curved and fingers like talons at the ready. His hands were usually so tentative. Over a millennium of this, displaced from what he'd once thought of as the "normal" flow of time, and Gerd had still never grown used to the feel of black oil oozing between his fingers.

Atticus used tools to kill them, but he almost seemed to respect the implements. Besides, Atticus also bought into the false excess provided by both the island and the pit, refusing to believe in the value of ignorance and simplicity.

You face what's hard, and you face it head on.

Personally, Gerd wasn't a big fan of the usual, tired approach. Applied to the Unwanted, it meant intimacy with even the foulest deeds. It meant looking them in the eye instead of just being done with them, the way Atticus sometimes did. It wasn't different from knowing the animal your meat came from. Or from having the decency to look a person in the eye as you killed them.

The pod shivered again, then opened like a blighted flower. The center was filled with the same flat black ichor as the pit creatures in which their seeds grew.

Gerd waited. Soon a small protrusion bloomed from the liquid. A small head, like that of an octopus, followed.

He usually sat back at this point, but his mind was elsewhere and it was impossible to relax or focus. He kept thinking of the blood in his coffee. And there was more; a storm seemed to be brewing, distant thunderheads making themselves a home on the eastern horizon. Atticus's wing was studded with rooftop weathervanes, and this morning they'd all been spinning in different directions.

So instead of sitting back he hovered, heart beating, and waited until the hatchling fully emerged.

It descended the pod's pimpled green side and landed on the tent's bottom, leaving tarry footprints with its six legs. It had a bulbous head, like the first soft breath into a limp balloon. It did not have eyes. A round opening yawned to display tiny triangular teeth, razor-sharp. This one seemed to have a tongue — unusual but not unheard-of. Seeing it ticked another nervous box inside him. Gerd didn't like to think of himself as superstitious, but he still saw an Unwanted's tongue as a bad omen.

He waited for the small thing to think at him. Usually they projected no fully formed concepts, only awful feelings that were impossible to describe. Staring down the message of an Unwanted was like studying a work of unsettling art

— all the more disturbing because nobody could articulate why it so unnerved them. Sometimes they gave off a sense of things crawling under the skin, or the flash of an innocuous image that was eerily wrong. Gerd remembered facing a worm-shaped Unwanted and getting a mental image of the back of his own neck, pocked with perfect holes. Eyes without any whites. Animals with spastic movement; a deer doing an impossible backbend while mewling in pain.

But today's first hatchling did not think. Instead it used that maggot-like tongue to speak with a phlegm-thickened voice.

And it said, "She died alone and screaming."

Gerd needed several seconds longer than usual to grab the thing, squeezing it until guts oozed between his fingers like paste.

She died alone and screaming.

He had no idea what that might mean, if anything.

Even after the rest hatched and Gerd dispatched them — even with half the afternoon's time to spare, he did not remove Atticus's construction or repair the porch. Instead he walked to the ocean, careful not to touch its lapping edge.

He looked into it. Down, not out.

Then stayed that way, for hours.

Chapter Six

Because the stranger, *you see, was a predator of sorts: a wolf who came dressed in sheep's clothing.*

The stranger gazed into a dark crystal ball to learn about the prince and princess, and hence he knew things about them that no one else did.

He knew that as happy as the princess appeared to be, she had a deep wound, there since birth: a certainty she hid every day that promised she would never be good enough — not for the prince, not for her subjects, not for anyone.

He knew the prince's great talent made him blind while under the spell of flattery, and that when the prince became occupied by his work, he would remain blind enough for the stranger to commit his dark deeds.

And lastly the stranger knew that as happy as the prince and princess appeared together, there was nothing in this world that, with sufficient lies and manipulation, could not be broken.

For months the stranger stayed in the castle with the prince and princess. He was always in plain sight to both, yet perpetually in hiding. He smiled at the prince, telling him the good word, while secretly whispering foul lies about the prince to his people, obscuring those untruths so nobody would know from whence they came.

He smiled at the princess, staying close, slowly casting a spell that would steal her heart.

And so the stranger worked under the surfaces to slowly pry them apart.

Chapter Seven

"I FOUND SOMETHING TODAY," Atticus said.

Gerd was darning socks. He'd conjured his entire wardrobe with nary a thought, and Atticus did the same with whole structures on a daily basis. Socks, however — like replacement cars and other arbitrary nouns — were a problem. Atticus said it was because they were meant to wear sandals like Greek gods. Gerd, on the other hand, preferred to keep his feet warm and blamed it on some rule-maker being an asshole.

Gerd had stationed himself in the common area. He would have preferred to do this kind of work in private, but the Authority seemed to want them together more often than not. Holing up and avoiding each other for too long had a way of turning his limbs transparent. It became difficult to walk. You forgot things, and thereby ended up wandering into common spaces anyway.

When Gerd didn't look up from his darning, Atticus made an annoyed grunt. He seemed to expect a reaction, and with good reason. New things were never *found* on the island. What you wanted to make, if you were able to make it, either happened with a modicum of control or was obvious in retrospect. What they'd previously believed to be "found" (significant objects unmade by them or the Authority) always turned out to have been created subconsciously or were presenting themselves out-of-order in time. It could take weeks, months, or years to realize a so-called found object had been known all along, its origin confused by the slippery, sometimes-backwards, often-suspended nature of time on the island.

A blank journal once discovered on the beach turned out to be Gerd's, for instance. He didn't know it until one day writing appeared inside, then began erasing itself one page at a time. He summoned the early, unmarked version of that same journal later on, filled the pages, then lost it along with the memory of ever having it. Only looking back did he see the *effect-then-cause* the journal represented.

Not *found. Discovered early.*

Atticus was either mistaken or lying.

Gerd reached for a spool of thread, pausing to flex his fingers on the arm of his throne-like chair. Atticus seized the opportunity by ramming a silver dagger between his phalanges, and pinning him to the wood.

"Do you mind?" Gerd snapped.

"Did you hear me? I said *I found something.*"

"A bottle cap? Beach glass?" Those things were garbage, and counted no more than rocks or trees. Both were plentiful, even though seashells were absent.

Well. Except that one time. Which was strange, because he'd been thinking of shells that day, of Shel, and—

"Something better." Atticus paused for drama, then added, "Something *real.*"

Gerd pulled the knife from his hand, cleaned it on his

pant leg, and went right back to darning. "You found nothing. It's a time-skipper."

"This isn't a time-skipper."

"Then it was left for you by the Authority."

"The Authority would never leave me such a thing."

If whatever he was talking about wasn't Atticus's out-of-time object, then perhaps it was Gerd's. "If it's mine, you cannot withhold it."

"It's not *your* relic, either." Atticus was grinning, enjoying this taunt that intrigued Gerd not at all.

Gerd sighed, feeling edgy and not especially himself. That was saying something since they both flitted in and out of consciousness from time to time, seldom feeling truly like any one thing. Gerd kept remembering the Unwanted and how it'd spoken to him earlier. He'd never heard one speak before, tongue or no tongue. Atticus surely would have mentioned if he'd seen anything like it.

"Listen to yourself," Gerd said. "There's nobody else here. Who would have dropped something for you to find? I've explored every corner of this island. There's no room to find a banyan tree, or a waterfall, or a—"

"It's none of those things. This is something ... *new*."

He sighed. "Leave me alone, Atticus."

"You fail to see what I'm saying."

"I see fine. I've just stopped caring. It's no doubt something you made without meaning to."

"You misunderstand."

"Idiot," Gerd said. "You create objects all the time in your sleep."

"This was not made in sleep."

Gerd resisted an impulse to rip through Atticus's pants and yank off his testicles. They grew back fast and could be plucked forever, like cherries from a magical tree.

"Oh?" He quelled his irritation and temper. "And what makes you so damn sure?"

Atticus seemed to have been waiting for this question. "I retrieved it with a stone."

Gerd tried not to show surprise. He failed.

"With one of the five stones you managed to give me this morning," Atticus continued. "It was a very *interesting* stone."

"Interesting how?"

"It was emerald green, with indigo imperfections."

Gerd blinked. All request stones ranged from white to black or the grays in between. There'd never once been any other color.

"*Now* I have your attention," Atticus said, seeing his face.

"You lie."

"I don't."

"Then what do you claim to have summoned with this wonderful stone?"

"I did not summon anything. I showed the stones to the Gatekeeper, and it was just as surprised. The stones were moss-covered when I took them from the lobster cage, but I'd swear all five were gravestone gray."

"You said green."

"Somewhere on the drive north, one changed."

"Ridiculous."

Atticus continued. "And once the Gatekeeper saw that green stone, it pulled me aside, away from the workers, into a cave I've never noticed before. And there I found it, in the chest of a creature."

"More lies." Gerd frowned, now furiously shaking his head. "Or more stupidity. If what you 'found' was inside a creature, then by definition it's an Unwanted."

"You're wrong. The thing I retrieved isn't *Unwanted* at all."

They stared at each other.

"How do you know?" Gerd finally asked, hating the feeling bubbling inside him.

"Because I *want* it." Atticus grinned, nice and wide. "Oh yes. I want it very much."

Chapter Eight

THE PRINCE FOUND glory in his art.

Commissions for his work multiplied and his stories grew in their infamy.

Yet a newly dark reputation teemed beneath it all. The prince was believed to be more sinister than he seemed, though he had not changed, and had done nothing wrong.

And at the same time, the princess excelled, but thanks to the stranger's manipulations, her inside wound — that dark thing inside her that had been held in check since childhood — also grew. Soon she suffered from dark moods, and only the stranger's words — no longer the words of her beloved husband — could cheer her.

And so it went, with the prince under one of the stranger's spells and the princess under another, until it was too late. The princess turned on her prince. She was angry with him, but he did not understand why.

The prince asked for his friend the stranger to advise him, but the stranger kept whispering lies:

She has grown sick.

She has grown sad.

She has, my friend, grown weary of you.

This last lie caused the prince great despair … but again, by the time he saw the fanciful twist of the stranger's hand, it was too late.

Chapter Nine

Sleeping in their wings would have made sense, but Gerd
had stopped trying to explain island happenings with logic
long ago. Beds placed in the wings did not persist, just like
body parts failed to persevere if their owners spent too
much time alone. Worse, separate beds sometimes turned
into piles of hog guts and heads overnight — never useable
meat.

And so it was always bedtime for them both. Sleeping
in shifts was too much of a hassle, and neither of them
were vampires. An unspoken cease-fire held a brittle peace,
defining sleeping hours as times when violence was
forbidden.

But Gerd was edgy and unable to rest. He flitted in and
out of dreams that seemed to come while he was awake,
lending them the character of visions. He relived the day's
events, seeing himself sipping the bloodied coffee, deciding
to leave the vault door open, and most of all watching that
first pod as it bloomed.

In brilliant detail, he repeatedly watched the black
finger emerge from its innards. He watched it climb down

its own discarded skin to cross the tent and tilt its head up at Gerd as if it could see him. He blanched at its yawning mouth, full of teeth that exceeded the allotted space. And its tongue was a ghastly sight, but nothing was more horrible than the voice, and what it said.

She died alone and screaming.

Diseased fluid sluiced between his fingers, Gerd again feeling the accompanying disconnect. Squeezing Unwanted hatchlings to death was usually cleansing. Murdering them felt almost meditative, and after a dispatching he always embraced his renewal.

But there was no meditative cleansing this time. Only unease and unrest.

He tossed. Turned.

Atticus is lying. He found nothing — especially not as a seed in the heart of a creature. We both know that's impossible, and he's a fool for expecting me to believe otherwise.

But despite the impossibility, Gerd couldn't shake a feeling that Atticus was telling the truth. He'd been intolerable throughout dinner, self-satisfied enough that he hadn't resorted to petty insults or violence. Atticus had seemed somehow *whole*. For once, he was not grubbing for imaginary desires, picking fights, or playing offense to defend his secret insecurities. He hadn't mocked Gerd. Or lingered at the table, seeking undelivered attention.

Manipulative, ethically corrupt, teasing son of a bitch …

Frustrated and exhausted, knowing the taboo but beyond caring, Gerd crossed to his adversary's bed. He pulled back the hangings, placed his palms on the other man's cheekbones, then used his thumbs to push through his eyes to the soft squish of brain. Once his thumbs found their maximum depth, Gerd pinned Atticus to the bed with a sword from the wall, then walked to the shed for a rotary saw.

"This is childish," Atticus said, with a wet gurgle in his throat, from the still-punctured lung.

Gerd shook his head, feeling an inexplicable wave of fury. "I told you this morning I'd dismember you in your sleep."

Atticus laughed, causing his chest to bounce on the blade. "Is that what this is about, Gerd? Fulfilling a threat?" He stopped, actually raising a fist to his chin in parody of The Thinker, even as he winced in pain. "Or have you broken our most precious rule for another reason? Are you jealous? *Afraid*, perhaps? Tell me, brother, *Have you done this because you believe me?*"

"You are a liar, Atticus. You have been a liar since the start of eternity."

"And when was that?"

The strange question stopped him, the saw still like a prop in his hands.

Atticus barged on before Gerd could speak. "How long do you feel we've been here? Do you honestly believe it's been forever?"

Gerd set down the saw, postponing the turning of one large Atticus into many small ones and instead taking hold of the sword already through his enemy and levering it down like a schoolroom paper-cutter. The new angle opened fresh wounds, but not enough to kill Atticus or knock him out. He screamed while holding his maddening smile.

"Why do you always play games?" Gerd gritted his teeth, speaking with a voice like gravel under heavy tires. He was rarely angry, but right now — after the day he'd had — he discovered his fury. Even the constant murder of his room-mate wasn't helping.

"It's our nature to play games," Atticus gurgled. "Does not the absurdity of our existence make that clear? It's obvious to me now, with my new, *Wanted* perspective."

"*Lies!* More lies!" Again Gerd levered the sword.

Atticus coughed, but seemed to be enjoying this. "If you saw the thing I found, you would understand."

"Then show me. Show it to me, so I can understand."

Atticus gave a little shrug. "You have not earned it, Gerdamene. It came *to* me and *for* me. Do you not see the joke? The absurdity of it all? What are the Unwanted, beyond things we do not want?"

"I give up. Tell me or live in agony forever."

Atticus struck him in the mouth. Teeth fell like white rain.

As Gerd reeled and lost his advantage, Atticus pulled down on the sword, trusting its forged edge to snap before bending. Once the handle was off, Atticus slid himself off the blade and grabbed a classic muzzle-loaded flintlock from the wall.

Gerd grabbed the other half of the set. They faced each other like colonial-era duelers.

"Go ahead," Atticus said. "Shoot me between the eyes. I'm fast enough to do the same to you before falling. And this is how we can live for the next millennium, in a constant state of death and rebirth. But the answer will still elude you."

"You have no more answers than I."

"That used to be true."

"And now?"

Atticus took a beat, then set the flintlock on an end table, daring Gerd to shoot him in the face even with his piqued curiosity. Then he said a strange thing: "What is that weapon you're holding?"

"*What?*"

"Humor me."

So Gerd did. "It's a 1700s-era dueling pistol."

"How long ago was that? The 1700s, I mean."

"I—" The answer had seemed obvious until he spoke.

"My vehicle. It's 1976, yes?"

"Yes …"

"And when was that?"

"It was …" But again, no answer.

"Seems I've had it for thousands of years, doesn't it?"

"You have," Gerd agreed.

"Of course. And that would make the year … what, by now? Is it 3976? 4976? Or is it less than that, and yet somehow you instantly knew its origin, its year, the reference it represents … all from a time that passed while you weren't even around?"

"Time is … different here."

"I see. Different how? Is there a ratio? A direction? Do you know?"

Gerd blustered. "You don't know either."

Atticus made a face that meant either *fair enough* or *shows what you know*.

He stepped closer to Gerd, putting his forehead to the tip of Gerd's pistol. He stayed that way for a while, then reached up and swiped the gun from Gerd's grip. Feeling weightless, Gerd did not protest.

"The Wanted is in my chambers," Atticus said in an ice-cold voice. "You desire it? *Then goddamn earn it for yourself!*"

He returned to his bed and pulled the hangings closed.

"I'll slit your throat the second you're asleep," Gerd said, unmoving.

But of course he wouldn't.

Not now.

Chapter Ten

Dark rumors *about the prince reached the princess's ears at exactly the wrong time — or the perfect time, according to the stranger's timetable.*

Word came that the prince had been unfaithful, though it was untrue.

Word came that the prince was full of lies, despite living as an open book.

Just as the princess teetered on the brink of the pit inside her, the prince became the last person she wanted comfort from. And so she fell, according to plan, into the waiting arms of the predator among them.

The distraught prince tried to win her back. He tried changing her mind — to erase what the stranger told her about him. But the interloper had done his work too thoroughly; already the world had turned against the prince as well.

He had his wealth and his fame … but the price, paid without his realization, was the hand of his bride.

Love and fortune spoiled like fruit left too long on the vine. The princess twisted as the stranger twisted her, until one day her soul finally turned black, inside and out.

She did not want the prince after that. She could see no good in him. She wanted only the stranger, whose every word she believed.

The princess knew she was brilliant, so long as the stranger said it was so.

She knew she was beautiful, because the stranger made her that promise.

She knew she had immeasurable value, despite the rotten place inside her, because under the stranger's sly counsel she'd come to believe it.

The princess was whole and the stranger was whole and the poor prince walked the world alone.

Chapter Eleven

A WEEK PASSED. Or perhaps more accurately, the sun rose and set seven times. Time was different here. But how? Was there a ratio?

They spoke little and ate every meal in silence, Gerd wary and Atticus smug. Something between them had changed. Atticus no longer lingered, dabbing his lips with one of the napkins that were always clean yet never washed, then leaving without a word.

Their vaults were in the basement, separated by another invisible membrane neither could cross. From his side, Gerd could see Atticus's vault but not the hatching tent inside nor any of its contents. Atticus must have visited his vault on the days of Gerd's turn at the pit to dispatch his new Unwanted, but it was not the vault that held his interest after dinner.

It was something in his chambers. Something over which Atticus obsessed, and Gerd could not reach.

In those seven long days, Gerd found himself preoccupied with matters that had never once engrossed him in the past. There was so much he'd never noticed, and so much he'd taken for obvious that, upon closer consideration, made no sense at all.

Gerd had grown used to thinking of the dock and lobster cage as south and the pit as north, which meant their little cabin on the water had to be facing east. Yet the waters beyond were where the sun set, not rose. Winds hit from all directions at different times. Weather approached almost instantly, never slowly over hours. Sunny days always seemed to bring cheery moods whereas rainy ones brought the sorrow, but now Gerd was starting to think things happened the other way around: first the feeling, then the weather.

The meat that constituted their entire diet (other than coffee, of course) appeared in a wooden box outside the door not unlike a compost bin, but only now was Gerd realizing that he'd never even once wondered where it came from or who put it there. Him not knowing how the meat arrived was one thing, but his total lack of curiosity about it was something else entirely.

Gerd used to be curious about things. So why hadn't he ever sat sentinel at the box, waiting to see who arrived? Electronics were imperfect here, but he might have tried summoning a camera to watch it, yet had never even once thought to do so.

And there was so much more — unexplained and unquestioned.

Why could some things be summoned but not others? Why did objects often appear that neither of them strictly wanted — and why did they only have to agree on *some* of what they summoned? It was like a joke, the arbitrary way the rules worked. A rigged shell game perhaps, where the proprietor always had an edge.

Where did the island end on the west side? Gerd realized with shock that he had no idea. It must end somewhere; the island's isolation was as axiomatic as the sun rising in the west and setting in the east. As the fact that yesterday followed today, and today followed all of the past at the same distance, and that his name was Gerdamene.

It *was* Gerdamene, wasn't it?

His mother, if he'd remembered her, would probably have given him that name whenever he'd possibly been born. Gerdamene or Larry. Or Lucius. Or Lonnie.

All of it, eternal and unquestioned. All of it, governed by rules that neither of them had been explicitly given but that both understood and always had.

Why had things been like this, for millennia on end?

How long do you feel we've been here? Do you honestly believe it's been forever?

A sick game emerged in which Gerd was alone on the board — appropriate, because although he and Atticus played often, their encounters were like deadly wagers, and never led precisely to death.

Each hour of every day that Atticus was away from the cabin, Gerd would walk to the boundary and, as before, try pressing himself through.

The first time he felt only resistance: that same repulsive force shoving him back to his side of the line.

The second and third time, he pushed harder, then harder. By doing this he discovered that the force was not entirely physical. His feet would lose traction if it was, and they didn't. So the repulsion was magical, maybe even mental. It was like being restrained by an invisible hand.

On the fourth try, he leaned into the barrier fully, head-forward and nearly horizontal. This time instead of being shoved back, Gerd's body obeyed gravity and fell forward.

It was progress, of sorts.

The next day he pushed again, armed with bruises and the knowledge that nothing was really there. Even knowing better, it was impossible to disbelieve the barrier. It still seemed to shove him, and Gerd lacked the strength of will to oppose it, despite knowing otherwise.

So he tried running at the barrier. He tripped as he crossed and fell, then sort of slithered backward in a way that might have been his own doing. Arms pushing while he didn't realize, toes hooking into the rug and pulling from the rear.

He meditated. Decided it was all in his head.

But nothing he tried made a difference.

By the one-week anniversary of Atticus's announcement, Gerd had decided several things.

First, he decided that what Atticus told him was either true or as good as true. Even if one of the stones Gerd's mind had forced into the cage for Atticus to retrieve hadn't turned green, Atticus at least believed that it had.

Second, if Atticus hadn't entered the pit and shown that stone to the Gatekeeper, who'd then ushered him into a special cave, then something equally odd had surely happened. Again: true or as good as true.

And lastly, even if Atticus hadn't slain a creature to retrieve the so-called "Wanted" in the same way they retrieved *Un*wanteds, he'd somehow procured a new thing in another way.

It all meant that what Atticus had told him could only be a half lie instead of a full one.

Whether the details of Atticus's story were accurate or not, a week's worth of change in Atticus's behavior made those details moot.

Something was changing his mood.

Something was driving him to obsession.

Something had granted Atticus knowledge he believed but that Gerd couldn't come close to understanding.

Something, most importantly, had unseated the balance

between them, sufficient that Atticus barely considered Gerd worth killing anymore.

And to think: The thing that had caused all their recent imbalance was right inside the cabin, inside Atticus's rooms. Though Gerd hadn't found a way to reach it, he could feel its presence from outside.

What's more, Atticus seemed to mean what he'd said about challenging Gerd to reach it. That bit was the strangest of all. The cabin or the Authority or something else was protecting the Wanted, not Atticus.

What had started as gloats were softer now. Tough love from Atticus, perhaps — a way of speaking that gilded the insults with an almost-inspiring edge.

I've accomplished something, Atticus's mood now seemed to say, *and if you work very hard, you can accomplish it too.*

Gerd was somehow keeping himself out of Atticus's rooms.

What was he missing?

On the seventh day he rested.

On the eighth day he decided.

The ninth day was his turn at the pit again, and for the first time in years there was only one stone in the lobster cage. He took it to the pit, to the Gatekeeper, and when the Gatekeeper's beetle lips said, *You take their fates into your hands,* Gerd replied by saying, *But whose fates are they really?*

The Gatekeeper seemed not to expect this. Its form relaxed, insects drifting from their assigned positions such that the thing's face became more like a featureless sphere. Then the features sharpened, a pair of centipedes rising into focused eyebrows.

"Follow me." And it took Gerd into a side cave he'd never seen, saying, "Choose."

The walls, floor, and ceiling of the new cave were teeming with creatures. It was lit only by the flickering orange of a mounted torch. The creatures saw Gerd and crawled forward on hooks and claws. Eyes flashed yellow and green and blue and red. Waiting. Lusting for his killing blade.

Gerd looked back. He said to the Gatekeeper, "Is this where you took Atticus?'

"It was not I who brought him anywhere," the Gatekeeper replied.

"Why today? What did I do differently today, that you took me here, too?"

"It was not I who brought you anywhere."

"My stone was black."

"Your stone was black," it repeated.

"His stone was green."

"His stone was green."

"Am I here to find something new?"

"Only one thing is ever truly new."

"I'm sorry?" Gerd said.

And the Gatekeeper, confusingly, said, "Exactly."

"Why am I here, in this new cave?" Gerd demanded, growing more impatient.

"Of that I cannot say, Gerdamene. Why *are* you here?"

One of the creatures approached closer than the others. It moved forward with purpose, like an offering. Gerd raised the Persuader Atticus had summoned into his pack, laying the single-occupancy trap on the stone floor behind him. He pointed his weapon at the creature and, unsure why, asked what it couldn't possibly answer.

"Are you the one?"

The twisted thing remained six-legged a few feet ahead, its chest rising and falling like an indolent accordion. Its ears were waxy and pointed. Its teeth were bone white and numbered in the thousands. The thing had openings all along its side that sighed from slits to sealed. *Ears? Gills?* Every one of them was different.

Gerd pulled the long lever on his weapon's side. The front of the Persuader shot forward on its cable and clamped over the creature's head, while the second line loosed whirring blades that sliced through its middle.

Gerd came forward and wrenched it open. Inside was a seed like any other, wiggling ever so slightly.

Gerd felt hatred. He felt wariness. There was nothing in this world he'd ever wanted to touch or hold or face less than the thing he'd be taking home now.

It wasn't Wanted, like Atticus's had been.

But he'd known that already, and his course of action lay elsewhere.

Chapter Twelve

But our sad story has yet to hit its lowest point.

One day, the stranger found another princess to pursue, and without so much as a mention he packed his bags and left the castle he'd claimed for himself.

The princess was left alone.

Left with all that hideous darkness now exposed inside her. The princess had no one to tell her she was clever. No one to tell her she was beautiful. No one to tell her she had value.

And so she came to disbelieve all of those things. The princess, who'd once lit the prairies with her smile, found herself worthless and alone.

One day she threw herself from the castle's highest parapet into a raging river below. The prince, who'd taken to watching the castle with forlorn devotion, saw it happen.

He rushed to the river, which was reachable without passing the castle gate. And there he found the princess, barely alive.

But he was present to hear her final words:

"We were happy, once ..."

Chapter Thirteen

GERD PUT the single Unwanted in his basement vault, adjusting the controls inside the tent to let it incubate. Then he took a seat and waited.

Nothing changed in the first hour. Or the second. Usually he just left the things overnight, so Gerd had no idea how long it took for them to hatch. After two hours his joints hurt. He brought a chair down from the foyer and continued his wait in comfort.

During the third hour, Gerd grew aware of a small emotion — one he didn't like, born from nowhere.

By the fourth hour, after a rushed and silent meal with Atticus, that nugget of unpleasant emotion had become a pond of anxiety. He looked over his shoulder every few seconds, certain he'd remembered something too late — a sense like leaving a roast in the oven to burn, or forgetting an animal in a locked car on a hot day.

By the fifth hour, back in front of the vault, his tired and bored mind slipped into hallucinations. His eyes fluttered closed, then jerked back open. A vision flickered in and out of his head. He might have been dreaming, but sometimes the sight was so real, it seemed to be right in front of him.

A person, indistinct and far enough away to obscure the details. Whoever-it-was sat half-slumped on a nonexistent couch, seeing as there was no other furniture in the basement. A sound came from the phantom — the kind of noise a person makes without realizing. It struck Gerd as the mewling of a wounded animal, or crying. The sound tore at his heart. Strangely, it made him feel guilty.

The sounds of misery echoed, and the vision came on like a light switch, filling his view before it went off, as if it had never even been there.

On.

And off.

The vision became clearer each time. It seemed closer to home with every passing second, though Gerd had no clue what it was.

The sounds grew louder, clawing his insides like so many nails on a chalkboard.

Then, startling him back to reality, movement caught his eye in the real world. It seemed the pod he'd been waiting for was finally opening.

Almost twenty hours ahead of schedule, the Unwanted he'd ripped from the eager creature was now in bloom.

INSTEAD OF KILLING it like he always did, Gerd took the vile thing in one hand and ascended the stairs. He half-expected Atticus to greet him, or ambush him, or have some witty taunt at the ready, but he had done something unusual at dinner, informing Gerd that he'd be alone for a while, because he, Atticus, was going back to the pit.

And that was appropriate. The strangeness of the evening.

Gerd's face was stone. He no longer saw the visions; they'd stopped when he'd taken the small, squirming thing from the pod. Unsure why he was doing so, he'd opened his hand to let the creature crawl up his arm. He grew squeamish and pulled back at the elbow, but then he stopped resisting and finally watched it roll and writhe in his palm with utter disgust.

It was foul. Loathsome. The very definition of *unwanted*.

But at the same time, it wasn't entirely unfamiliar.

Now, standing before the boundary into Atticus's share of the cabin, Gerd paused with his fist closed loosely around the thing. He no longer remembered where this idea had come from, despite it being fewer than five minutes old. He similarly had no clue why he'd thought it would work.

Why *would* it? Or really, how *could* it? Things on the island *never* changed. It had been this same endless cycle forever.

The Unwanted looked like a large scorpion coated in tar. Its tail had taken on a hook in the short trip upstairs, and even carried a small, sharp barb.

Gerd thought: *If you don't dispatch it now — if you don't squeeze this thing out of existence enough that you'll never need to see it again — then you'll be stung. And there will be unending, unendurable pain. The kind of agony you will regret forever.*

He faced the barrier.

He looked down at the horrid thing clawed from a demon's chest, apparently now his pet for eternity. It lay flat in his palm as he watched, tiny legs twitching, seeming to beg for Gerd to finally end it.

But he wouldn't.

With the thing in his hand, Gerd stepped through the barrier. This time, it offered no resistance.

Once through, when Gerd looked down at his palm, the Unwanted was gone.

HE WAITED two minutes just to be sure.

But nothing pushed him out of Atticus's chambers. Or threatened to pluck Gerd from his trespassing, sending him from rooms he should not have entered.

And that was strange, but not as strange as it should have been. Gerd felt somehow different in this place. His mind was everywhere but here, patrolling the past and investigating the future, dreaming fancies that never seemed to have happened.

He felt like he was losing his mind as he stood just past the border, neither advancing into Atticus's rooms nor retreating to his own. Voices came. Sights came. His thoughts were BINGO balls in a hopper, leaping hither and yon.

He flashed to his vision from the basement, knowing it was a non-thing and yet somehow familiar. And he thought, *Let it go. It wasn't real.*

But he didn't buy that. Somehow, it *was* real — just … not for Gerd.

So why was it dogging *him*, if it wasn't his? Why did it make him feel so bad? Was it another cruel joke, like the constant knives piercing his back? Did the vision perhaps belong to Atticus — a new way for his opponent to torment him?

Forget the visions. You're here because you're a criminal. It's not stillness of mind that let you pass the barrier. It's not anything with the Unwanted, either — the way you acknowledged instead of denying it. So greed must have made the difference. You're here because you want to steal. Because you're a criminal. Selfishness that compels you. Greed tugs at your leash.

But no. Gerd was not cursed with greed. For Gerd, the island was a place to want nothing — to accept what came instead of scrabbling for *more and more* like Atticus always did. *Not thinking*: that was the ticket.

And yet Gerd couldn't deny that things *had* changed. They'd always had parity — a perfect balance of power and knowledge. He and Atticus, as far as he remembered (which he didn't), had always been two hairs in a braid. But now that perfect balance had tipped. If this was a game to win, Atticus now seemed to be in the lead.

"Balanced?" mocked Atticus's whisper. *Balanced for what purpose, Gerd? What do you think we are here on this island to do? What do we protect? What is so valuable that we must constantly war against one another, preventing its escape or exploitation? It's all a lie, Gerdamene; do you really not see that? We tie knots in the mind, always working a puzzle between our ears. To solve it is our nature, not to* guard *it. Although, that's not true for you, is it, Gerd? You prefer the jumble to a puzzle solved, so you don't have to look it in the eye. Or have you forgotten?*

Gerd ignored the voice. He knew why he was here.

The Authority compelled Gerd, which meant the Authority compelled them both.

Their purpose was as plain as the sky above. As plain as the winding dock. As the decrepit, mismatched cars in the driveway that had been here for as long as Gerd could remember, since the very dawn of time.

And how long ago was that, Gerd — the dawn of time? Were you born on this island? Did you even have *a birth?*

Gerd finally managed to stop the voice. If he didn't quit pondering in the insufferable, overthinking way Atticus pondered, he'd go crazy.

His thoughts turned to the Wanted instead, which Gerd realized he could now feel like a presence. The Wanted was just where Atticus said he'd find it. It made him wary. Because what could the "Wanted" be, if not an Unwanted that Atticus had yet to slaughter? What did Unwanted become, anyway, if allowed to persist?

He reached a door. Same as the others, but from inside came an energetic pulse like a heartbeat.

It's here. The thing is right here, *inside this room.*

He pushed the door open to a chamber, hosting a couch, a desk, and little else.

A young girl sat on the couch, maybe six years old but small for her age. She wore a simple white dress and had full, robust hair. Her bare feet did not reach the floor, swinging them lightly, nudging the couch with her heels.

"Hello," she said. "My name is Shelby. Would you like to play a game?"

Chapter Fourteen

AND SO THE STORY CONCLUDES, but it need not end in sorrow.

For there is a lesson to this tale, and in its way, a happy ending.

A darkened soul cannot survive the flight to Heaven, see. What ascended, when the princess left her mortal body, was the being of light she'd always been.

And so she waited, watching, for the prince.

He would live a very long time, but at the end of that time, he and his princess would be together again.

LUCAS CLOSED the storybook and looked at his daughter, awaiting her verdict.

"Is that it?" she asked him.

"What, you want more?"

"Well, it's not a very satisfying ending, is it?"

Lucas was used to this, her always saying what she meant, just like her father. "How so?"

"You didn't say that they lived happily ever after, Daddy. That's how a story's supposed to end."

Lucas laughed. Oh, yeah. He could add that, saccharine-sweet though it was. "You're right. *They lived happily ever after.* I'm sorry. My grownup stories don't end that way, so sometimes I forget."

She cocked her head. "Grownups aren't happy in the end?"

Now, how should he answer that little gem? "Let's worry about that when you're old enough to read those stories. Deal?"

She considered him with an expression beyond her years, then slid down into the covers like a letter into an envelope. "How old?"

"Maybe twelve for the first. Think you can wait that long?"

"But that's *twice* my age!"

"Twice, huh? You could get a jump on math right now."

She made a face. Math was boring.

"Which book would I read first?"

"*Delilah.* It's young adult, but you're already kind of an adult."

The girl laughed.

"Not adult enough to date, though."

She laughed harder. Lucas, knowing that any great performer should end on a high note, stood from her bed. His hand was on the light switch when she stopped him.

"Daddy?"

"Yes, sweetheart."

"I did like most of your story. But did she really have to die in the end?"

Her expression went beyond curiosity. The fear of mortality, perhaps, and for that Lucas could hardly blame her.

He sighed, then returned to her bedside. "I don't control the stories, Shelby. Remember how I told you that?

They come to me how they come to me. And in this one … yes, the princess died." He rushed on; *the princess died* was about as grim a sentence as you could say out loud to a kid — on par with charging Kermit with sexual misconduct. "But that's the story behind the story, see? The moral?"

"You mean the lesson."

"That's right."

"And what *is* the moral of the story, Daddy?"

Well, shit. He couldn't answer that for the same reason this particular test audience proved the need for script changes. The moral was supposed to be that every person is in control of her choices and hence her own life, but it probably came off as *The princess made her bed, so she had to lie in it.* You couldn't end a children's tale by blaming the victim, even when blaming made sense.

"The moral is that Daddy should tweak the ending, I guess."

He thought she might persist, but the question only left a shadow on her features.

"You okay, kid?" He should have started a new thriller instead of this little ditty. He'd meant to create something lighthearted, but of course it'd come out charred.

"I guess."

"*You guess?*" Lucas leaned in, trying for playful. "Well, I *guess* maybe I'm a frog."

"You're not a frog, Daddy."

Lucas rose again, his hand back on the switch when the girl spoke again.

"Daddy?"

"It's bedtime, hon. Enough talking for now."

But that look was still on her face. Oh, God — had he screwed up, with this edgy take on a tired genre? And in trying to be new, had he scarred his daughter same as her mother had? How old would she be when Shelby first told her therapist, *After Mommy died, Daddy started scaring me?*

"Sweetheart. What is it?"

"It's the princess."

"Princess went to Heaven. And in Heaven, she and the prince were rid of all their troubles on Earth. Don't you see?"

"Yes, but …"

"But what?"

"She didn't die when she fell, did she? Not right away."

Oh. Yeah. Lucas forgot why he'd written it that way, though that detail had seemed vital at the time.

Shelby's eyes were haunted when she continued, speaking words a child naive of trauma would never say — and in that moment, his quiet worry for her multiplied.

Every day felt the same now, and for Lucas that had meant moving on. For the girl, moving on might not be so easy.

"The princess," she told him. "She died alone and screaming."

Chapter Fifteen

GERD COULDN'T SPEAK.

He literally could not remember the last time he'd seen a person other than Atticus. It was another of those weird internal schisms, like how he knew all about his adversary's car without any direct memories or experiences to offer him the knowledge. He remembered people just fine, it was an intellectual understanding: *People live with people; people interact with people; that's how life is.* But still, it felt to Gerd like that knowledge had come from a book.

"How are you here?" he asked.

The girl gave a little shrug — a confident, *because-that's-how-it-is-dummy* gesture that he'd seen on Atticus a thousand times. He considered her again, bearing in mind that she couldn't be what she seemed. No one came to the island, just like nothing here was truly found, or new. If this strange girl-shaped thing was in Atticus's quarters, it had to be the Unwanted (the Wanted) he'd been taunting Gerd about. Nothing else could upset the order they'd held here for thousands of years.

But had it really come from a pod? Was *this* what happened if you let them grow?

"I'm here the same as you're here," said the girl.

"I was *always* here. *Atticus* was always here."

"And *I* was always here," she echoed.

"No." Gerd shook his head. "He found you a week ago."

"*Found.* But I was always here."

"You weren't."

"I was."

Gerd considered a response, then turned on his toe without a word. This was too much. He'd expected to find a bauble — maybe a toothy pet in an aquarium. Never had he expected any interaction with the thing.

"Where are you going?" the girl called.

But Gerd was gone. Down the hallway, around the bend, toward the stairs. A barrier at the bottom, with comfortable familiarity beyond it. The girl's small, barefoot steps slapped on the ground behind him.

"Wait!"

He took the bannisters under his palms and skipped down the steps, hitting every third or fourth.

"Wait! You have to tuck me in!"

His head began spinning. The landing below was slowly rotating. The edges of his vision were fuzz. His body remembered the feeling: he was about to pass out.

Everything upended. Gerd's scrabbling feet, previously so confident, lost all their tension a quarter inch above their last step. The final landing skidded to one side, his right ankle rolling. The left-side wall screamed by like lightning. The floor was right behind it, slamming Gerd in the ear.

His vision swam, now from vertigo and concussion. He forgot where he was.

At home, yes? And it's game night, yes?

The living room was ahead. And the couch they should have burned. What happened to that couch, and why was it still there? He didn't want to look at it.

Small bare feet padded into Gerd's line of sight. He tried to look up but either his neck was broken or he'd forgotten how to move it. He rolled his eyes instead, able to see only as high as her knees where they disappeared into her dress.

"Don't go yet," she said from above him, "not while we still have time to play."

GERD PEEKED UP AT ATTICUS.

Shoulders hunched. Knots in his muscles. His injuries were all healed by now, and that meant Gerd was causing his own pain moment by moment. He had a fork in one hand, a knife in the other. He used the latter to push food onto the former, hoping to finish his meal posthaste.

"How was your day, friend?" Atticus asked, with a lilt in his voice, as if a joke waltzed between them.

"Average."

"*Average*," Atticus repeated. So clearly he knew. The girl must have told him, seeing as she was real and alive and had a mouth with which to do so. There was a long silence. Eventually, tired of waiting, he spoke again. "I've been thinking."

"Have you."

"We should take a trip."

"To where?" Gerd asked.

"To anywhere, as long as it's away from this place."

Gerd looked down, dragging meat through meat sauce and pretending it was bread.

"You think I'm joking," said Atticus.

"I think you're delusional. There is the cabin. The cage. The pit."

"Yes, those. But we've never tried to ignore them. Never once turned our backs."

"Are you suggesting we stop collecting demands? Stop going to the pit?"

"Yes."

Gerd laughed. "You're insane."

"I'm not sure I am, Gerd." Atticus pretended to look at a watch, but his wrist was naked. "I wonder. It's null o'clock. Are you previously engaged? Planning a big night of darning socks and pulling your pud?"

"Fuck off, Atticus."

"Because if you can find the time in your schedule, there's something you should see."

Danger signs flared. Internal klaxons brayed warnings. *The girl.*

Gerd had been thinking about her for hours. Trying to believe she wasn't there, because how could she be? They knew the island's rules. They knew the way things had to be, for this fragile balance to endure.

The girl changed everything, so she couldn't be real.

"I don't need to see anything." Gerd shook his head in defiance.

"You were so curious yesterday."

"Mmm ..."

"And the day before. And the day before that."

"I've decided to accept that which I cannot change."

Atticus leaned forward, rising slightly, one elbow on the table. "And what of things you *could* have changed?"

Gerd kept his eyes down, out of food but pretending to chew anyway.

Atticus laughed. "You are such an enigma."

"How so?"

"You are curious only about the things you wish to believe. A poor scientist, theorizing only on your favorite happenings."

"And how are you, Atticus?"

"I wish to know it all. Good or bad. Desired or loathed. I would rather live in the light than the dark."

"*You.*" Gerd laughed this time. "*You* are the illuminated one? *You*, who covets material comforts that aren't even there. You who thrives on excess. You, whose lust allows our world to persist."

"Really, Gerd? You told me our only real power was in denial."

"I meant the denial of impulses. The holding back of animal instincts. Not the denial of …" But there was no end to that sentence.

"I see. So you are open, then. You are willing to threaten your worldview, and question all you hold true."

"What I hold true *is* true."

"Then come with me," Atticus said, "and prove it."

THEY STOOD at the lip of the pit in twilight. The garish sore in the earth glowed red — same as the sunset now only moments away. From the right angles, the horizon appeared as a slash, rather than as a separation of air and ground.

"Sit and watch."

Atticus sat.

After a few seconds, Gerd followed.

As twilight deepened, he could see sprites dancing on the shimmering membrane that formed the pit's upper lip: small, ghostly white blurs that could have been anything. For the first few seconds they seemed to be a trick of the eye, but the longer he sat, the more Gerd saw the variety of shapes among the sprites. Some were small things, like trinkets. Some formed blobs, swelling into larger blobs before evaporating. Others appeared to have legs. Torsos. Heads.

They assembled on the membrane, growing until they were substantive enough to rise.

"It started today," Atticus told him. "At first I thought I was seeing things. I spotted them from the corners of my eyes, never straight on. After a while I gave them all my focus, but that made them vanish. They want to hide. See?"

Atticus pointed. Gerd watched sidelong as another human-shaped glow rose, looked their way, then zipped off once it seemed to notice them looking.

"This is why I came back to the pit. They grew clearer as the sun moved lower. I could see them proper once I put the sun behind me. The closer it came to twilight, the easier they were to see. And they can't see *us* as well in this, either."

Gerd looked over. "You aren't saying they're conscious."

"I'm only saying that they are new." He tipped his head thoughtfully. "Or old."

Gerd considered the shapes. They were like smoke escaping an almost-sealed container. "What's it mean?"

"Maybe nothing." Atticus shrugged.

But Gerd knew he didn't believe that. Atticus had wanted Gerd to see this. *Needed* him to see it.

Gerd watched. Waited.

"There's more." Atticus rose, and Gerd guessed he was supposed to follow.

They walked until they reached the down-sloping spot past their usual parking area: the place where they always entered the pit with their stones and left with their bounty.

But something was different now. Past the slope was a large fissure, a crack in the bedrock that descended into what looked like forever.

Gerd straddled it. There was red, lava-like fluid at the bottom.

"This opened while I was here. There are others." Atticus pointed vaguely. "All of them opened at once, like the snap of fingers. About a half hour before I returned, I imagine." He looked meaningfully at Gerd. "Did anything happen at the cabin today?"

Gerd shook his head, but yes, something had happened.

He had woken face-up in the foyer just as Atticus opened the door. He remembered because Atticus "accidentally" dropped one of the lodestones on his neck. Gerd didn't know how long he'd been unconscious or why he hadn't ended up back near Atticus's rooms, but it didn't feel like he'd been out for long. Maybe twenty minutes. And if so, then he'd seen the girl around the same time the cracks opened.

Rock shifted underfoot. Atticus scrambled away as Gerd stepped back.

Together they watched the fissure widen, the rock on which they'd been standing crumbling down into the depths.

"The pit is collapsing," Atticus said.

Chapter Sixteen

SOMEONE WAS SHAKING LUCAS.

His head hurt. His neck was a wet noodle, his skull stuffed with Pop Rocks. If it wasn't his hangover attacking, then surely the apocalypse was nigh.

"Lucas? LOGAN!"

He opened his eyes to see Miranda's face.

"Jesus. You okay?"

She still had his shirt at the collarbones. She wasn't nudging him like a man who needed waking, she was harassing him like a kid in need of some slapping-around.

"You hear me? You okay?"

He turned his head and groaned. He managed to half sit up, then propped himself up on an elbow. "What's up?"

"*What's up?* It's ten thirty."

"At night?"

She sighed, let go, then stood. He fell back immediately. Moving was impossible. Everything hurt.

"What?" he asked.

"No, not *at night.* Ten thirty in the morning. On a workday. Remember work?"

He rubbed his face.

"Hell, Lucas. What's wrong with you?"

"Nothing's wrong with me."

"You weren't answering your phone."

"I was sleeping."

"I've been trying to wake you up for five solid minutes. I thought you were comatose. I thought you were *dead*."

Lucas tried to roll his eyes. That hurt, too. "I'm late."

"Are you even listening to me?" Miranda demanded.

He tried to stand, but that hurt most of all.

"Tell me you were attacked," she said when he flopped back onto the couch. "Tell me you were poisoned. Tell me you didn't just get *so fucking high* that I couldn't wake you."

Lucas groaned, then realized something and bolted upright. "Where's Shelby?"

"At school."

"Did you take her?"

Miranda's pretty face was full of disappointment and scorn. "She took the *bus*, Lucas. Hours ago. Right on time, like a champ, while you were lying here in your own filth."

"My own …?" He stopped, spying the bile-colored spill across one of the cushions. Dried chunks were laid out like breadcrumbs, leading the way to a pile of empty bottles.

"She fell on the playground. No big deal, just a scrape, but the school has to let you know. The nurse tried calling you." Miranda pointed at his phone, not two feet from his head — with the ringer at full volume, no less. "They called your work number when you didn't answer. I went next door to your office and answered after the second time, thinking it might be Markovian Industries. Then I thought something like this might have happened once I knew it was the school. So I took care of it by telling them I was your wife."

"You—?"

"They believed me, Lucas. Why would they believe me?"

"I guess because you sound like her?"

"You know what I mean."

Lucas rose, ignoring her.

"Where are you going?"

"To take a shower."

"Now?"

"Isn't that why you're here? So you can get me off to work?"

"Fucking hell, Lucas."

"I have to take a goddamn shower if I'm going to work!" Lucas snapped, then under his breath he added, *"Nag."*

"Excuse me?"

"I said *you're a nag*, Miranda," he spat, not feeling quite himself. "This is who you met. This is who I am. I didn't ask for your help."

"Jesus, Lucas. Five minutes to wake you. *Five minutes!* But I guess the problem is just me, nitpicking your wonderful life choices." She stabbed a hand at his phone again. "You have a daughter who depends on you! I talked to the nurse, and to *Shelby*. Then we had the weekly roundup at the office. You were supposed to present. Of course Roger flipped when you weren't there. He started right in about how he's had it with you, and that 'this is the end for Lucas Fucking Latham.' I told him you were griev-ing. I stepped in and stood up for you since I think you deserve some slack—"

"Goddamn right I do."

"Oh. I see." She put her hands on her hips. "This is just a service for you. Something I'm expected to do, as the next in line."

"I don't need your insecurities right now, Miranda."

"Just my help, right? Just a stand-in as substitute parent to the asshole I happen to be fucking?"

Lucas turned his back and walked away. Last night had been particularly hard. He'd tried to rework his little fairy tale after Shelby went to bed, slightly horrified when he read it back and realized how it must have sounded to a six-year-old.

The princess played with fire, so the bitch got burned.

His cautionary tale had become so macabre.

Shelby had taken longer than usual to fall asleep, and Lucas's good-dad cheer began to wane once the sky was as black as the things that kept squirming inside him. Nights had always been hard. Nighttime was when he felt most alone, even back when Kate was merely away, visiting her mother. The house was so big and vacant now, once Shelby was sleeping. Staying by her bedside kept him staring out the windows, and suffering under an umbrella of dread.

By the time he returned to his home office last night, Lucas was in no mood to execute surgery on a tale that was supposed to be lighthearted. But he needed something to fill his time, and didn't want to resume his other in-progress story, about a serial killer without any conscience. He found a simple solution to his dilemma by going from beer to whiskey, then to a copious amount of weed. Somehow he'd remained upright long enough to revamp the children's story, though he was frightened, from that angry and intoxicated state, to see how it now read.

He didn't remember coming out to the living room. He didn't like sitting on the couch, let alone sleeping on the thing. It felt like someone else had moved him.

He emerged from the shower and found Miranda still there.

"Oh, for fuck's sake."

"You're welcome," she replied.

"I didn't ask you to stay. I didn't want you to stay. *I don't need anyone right now; do you hear me?*"

"Just like always, huh?"

"Really, Miranda? You want to do this now? Why don't we light some candles for a romantic dinner. Cop a squat and discuss our relationship."

She plunked down three feet from his puddle of sick. "Actually, yes. I *do* want to do this now."

"I was kidding."

"This isn't just about you. It's me, too. How do you think it feels, to think back on all the times she cried on my shoulder? Cried *about you*?"

"That's your issue, not mine."

"Yeah. I guess it is." Miranda nodded, frustrated tears already falling. "But I shouldn't have to do it alone. I can't tell anyone else. You get that, right? How it would look …"

"Miranda … Not now."

"I'm sorry?"

"I said *not now!*"

Lucas moved from bathroom to bedroom, grabbing his slacks, shirt, and tie.

Miranda stood behind him like a creature, a twisted authority over things he'd already handled, while he composed his hair in the mirror.

"She was my friend, God damn you."

"She was my wife."

"*Was.* Just like that."

"Yes!" He turned to look at Miranda instead of her reflection. "Just like that! I loved her, but she was sick. And—"

"Sick."

"Yes, *sick*! By the end she was popping Klonopin like Certs. She was a zombie. And—"

"Popping them because of us."

"She didn't know about us."

"How many of the others *did* she know about?"

Lucas finished in the bathroom, grabbing his briefcase from the office at a speed walk, Miranda still on him like glue.

"We're having this conversation."

"No, we're not."

"Yes, we are!"

He spun around again, and this time his hand seemed desperate to hit her. He never would, but rage was still a glowing red poker in his mind. They were nearly nose-to-nose when he settled.

"You need to start talking to me," she said.

"I'm fine. I don't need anything."

"Not for you. We need to talk *for me*, Lucas!"

"*For you*," he repeated.

"You owe me that."

"Why?"

"I've been your goddamn maid. Your babysitter. Your cook. You're not a helpless person. I've seen how much gusto you throw yourself into things you actually give a shit about. But I guess I should understand, right? After all, she was *only your wife*."

"So you're saying I don't care?"

"I'm saying you're a coward."

They faced each other for what felt like a very long time.

Then Lucas picked up his briefcase and swept right by her, out to the garage without looking back.

Chapter Seventeen

GERD WOKE the next morning with the feeling that it had all been a dream.

The pit had been there, of course, reaching long tendrils from its depths to drag him down into its maw. But beneath that — hidden from view — awaited an even blacker fate.

He avoided Atticus, using one of the side doors. He took his empty pack and started his truck. By the time he'd arrived at the south dock, the pack was full, but not overly so. Gerd almost wished it was heavy. The light load Atticus had given him felt a little too much like a cookie.

Last night had been strange. So unlike their usual ways.

Atticus had plenty of theories on their ride home, and kept jawing on about them into Gerd's silence. Things had changed on the island before, he said — evolution was life's only constant. Gerd, who remembered no changes, remained mute.

What had shifted, other than the abomination of that girl?

There was Gerd, there was Atticus, there was the judgmental, nagging rule of the Authority; there was the land and the water and the cabin and two vehicles that felt like a joke. The same as it had always been.

Nothing perturbed the island's immortal certainty.

The pit? Collapsing? Not possible. The pit too was eternal. It had been here when they arrived — which was either forever ago or so long ago that no one could remember. It was, and would always be, their burden to carry.

Gerd had accepted his duty: to serve the infernal pit in exchange for peace.

But now it seemed Atticus felt differently.

We need to leave, he kept insisting on their way back to the cabin. *Don't you see? The* surface *is collapsing, but the guts are growing, rotting the world beneath us like a rotting apple core. Look at the pattern of fissures, Gerdamene. The pit won't collapse into nothing. It will devour everything. Eventually there will be no grounds for us to live on. It will keep spreading until the guardian's domain is all that is left of our island. Until we, and everything that exists here, is gone forever.*

Gerd had replied with a grunt of disbelief, and one simple question: *How could you possibly know that?*

And Atticus had said, *I see it in the Wanted.*

Meaning the little girl who had no business being here. The girl who had spoken to Gerd that day, unafraid of him, wanting or perhaps needing to play a game.

I know you've been to see her, Gerd! Atticus shouted after him back at the cabin — Gerd marching hard for his quarters, determined to sleep there no matter what it cost him. *You passed the barrier, didn't you? What further proof do you need that it's all coming to an end — one way or another?*

He slept. He woke. In the morning, before stepping into the truck, he'd heard a rustling in the woods. He followed when it repeated, thinking it might be an animal, despite an absence of game on the island. But the noise wasn't a buck or a bear or even a squirrel. It had come from a large crack in the bedrock. At the bottom of the new chasm, below crisscrossing roots, there was now a river of molten rock.

Gerd had looked up, standing at the fissure's end and sighting toward its source. Snaking north, toward the pit, though things couldn't have possibly spread that far.

The guts are growing, rotting the world beneath us like the core of a bad apple.

But that was a lie. The island was a protected place, not sinister. That's how it was meant to be.

So he'd ignored it. Got into his car and drove. The pack Atticus filled for him contained only a handheld Extractor, sufficient to kill creatures that lay at his feet … which had now happened twice in the pit's heart.

More evidence of evolution in this unchanging place — and one more thing for Gerd to try and ignore. He told himself to keep working.

Or I could swim away. Just drop this whole stupid thing, get wet, and paddle until I reach land. Or until I die. Either would be preferable to this.

Now on the dock at the island's southern end, the shark's enormous fin surfaced, then neared. It rose higher as the predator slid nearly all the way onto dry land. It lay breathing, massive gray sides expanding and collapsing like a bellows. Its head was forward and unable to turn, but the single black eye Gerd could see clearly warned him away from what he had been considering.

Gerd offered it a single nod, promising he wouldn't execute on his impractical, pointless flights of fancy. The shark still waited, watching his ritual as if for the first time ever. He forced himself to ignore the shark, working fast as he reeled up the line.

Gerd found only one stone in the lobster cage. It was white, which meant an easy kill and removal.

He showed it to the Gatekeeper, and the creature's beetle lips nearly sighed.

"You won't see," it said.

"I don't know what you're talking about."

"You won't see," it repeated.

Gerd returned to the truck with his small burden retrieved and found something unnerving. He'd parked far from the spreading network of fissures: those crisscrossing weaves of red and black that resembled a spider's web. One of the drive wheels was now hanging over a miniature chasm. Cracks in the ground surrounded the truck in a giant gramophone bell. Another piece of rock fell as Gerd watched, and through the hole he saw directly into the chamber from which they claimed the things they were bound by the Authority to claim: the Unwanted, snatched from the deep and denied life on the surface. And now, thanks to the cracks, they could see the surface, opening like a blighted flower.

Gerd shifted the truck into four-wheel drive so he could back away from the hole.

"The pit's not spreading," he said to himself. "Not at all."

THE GIRL JOINED them for dinner over Gerd's protests.

He ignored her. Ignored *it*.

This was less a person than a clot of wretched memory.

But Shelby, to Gerd's right, was dressed well for a clot. Her blue dress was new, and had either been summoned by Atticus, or she had somehow summoned the garment herself. Her hair — washed, blown dry, and curled —

hung in brown ringlets. A blue bow, to match the dress, was perched atop her head. And her half-sized chair was a perfect scale model of their usual thrones.

Obnoxiously, it was stationed close to Gerd's. A private dinner for two, if they ignored Atticus at the end.

"Why is it here?" Gerd nodded to the thing beside him.

"So that you remember."

"I don't need to remember. It's not mine." Gerd shook his head. "You extracted it. That means it's yours."

"Some things belong to us both."

"Daddy Gerd," said the girl, "will you please pass the butter?"

"There is no butter."

But somehow today, there was. There were all her favorite things, from the toast on her plate to all those jams and jellies, and the big square slices of cheese.

"Have some," said the girl, indicating the toast.

Gerd steeled his gaze, refusing to give it the satisfaction of acknowledgement.

He wouldn't look — not at the girl-thing, not at the new foods, not out the window at the red glow from the lava-rich fissures. He would not look at Atticus most of all. His adversary had gone from arrogant to weak, and now lived to observe Gerd, waiting for some sign that Gerd himself could not foresee nor imagine.

Days passed.

The girl-thing became a fixture of their routine. Gerd avoided the common areas when they were occupied because everything now felt like a parody of family: life lived on a cheesy sitcom, perhaps. Atticus played father while the thing pretended at childhood. It was now almost normal-size. Atticus used its chosen name, and feminine pronouns like that wasn't a lie. The foyer felt like a play-room, with unusual objects summoned or suddenly provided from nowhere. There were dolls and building kits. Books, for the precocious thing loved to read.

"Tell me a bedtime story, Daddy Gerd," it would say from time to time, when he could no longer avoid the common spaces. "Tell me a story, then put me to bed."

Because her bed, too, was now in the sleeping room. An oasis between Gerd and Atticus's four-posters, draped with a sage-green bedspread and lined with stuffed animals that had appeared from nowhere.

Gerd ignored it.

"Please, Daddy Gerd?"

"Go to Hell." Because that's pretty much where the thing had come from.

"Please?"

And at that point Gerd would relocate — to his rooms if he hadn't already spent too much time there, or at least to another part of the shared area. Either way she would give up and approach Atticus. Then Gerd heard her say, "Tell me the story about the princess who died."

On the fourth day, Gerd accepted that Atticus could, and would, maintain this farce forever. It was his newest and greatest form of torture: subtle, brilliant, and horrible. Enough to make Gerd miss being drawn and quartered by his foe. He missed impalements and bisections. He missed decapitation — especially the tries where the implement used failed to sever the spine. He missed being mauled to death on repeat. This smug, mindfuck torture was so much worse in every way.

So on that fourth day, Gerd ceased his protests. He did not shoo the girl-thing away as before, nor did he shout or move his chair, or shove her toward Atticus's side of the dinner table.

Halfway through the first meat course, it rose.

She rose.

Shelby rose.

And without a word, she wrapped her short arms as far as she could around Gerd's middle. The movement practically laid her in his lap.

"I don't blame you," she said. "I don't hate you."

Gerd, for reasons unknown, thought he was going to cry.

Chapter Eighteen

WORK, sleep, repeat.

Work, sleep, repeat.

Something was different — some foul thing metastasizing in a mental place Lucas couldn't reach. He combatted the mystery with enforcement of routine. Familiarity and stability cured everything. When nothing changed, there were no loose ends and nothing to fret about. If he rested his boat in glassy waters, then only he could rock it, or pitch himself into the drink.

Lucas stopped boozing, not wanting to give Miranda an excuse to nag him. For the same reason he stopped smoking weed, and started setting two alarms every morning. After work, he had dinner with Shelby and they made jokes and played games. He read the more appropriate of his side-hustle stories out loud whenever she requested it. Then he'd write for a while once she was sleeping.

But those new words spilled onto the page without coherence, characters like insects crawling under his skin.

His sleep was as fitful as his writing, and each day would repeat.

Until Saturday, when a lack of a formal workday shattered his routine in a way he should have anticipated but didn't.

Saturday's alarm startled him from a dream he could almost remember — some horrid vision involving elements from Shelby's favorite game. He woke unsettled but unable to remember why, the dream taunting him from under three layers of consciousness.

He put his feet on the floor and plodded to the bathroom. The alarm was the same; its purpose was not. Something about the incongruity gave Lucas a troublesome flutter. For a scant moment he distinctly felt that he *had* no purpose.

Disoriented, he stared at his reflection, mired in the present. Suddenly there was no past or future. There was only this single moment, *right now,* and in it Lucas was pointless and alone. Without the need for a getting-ready routine on Saturday, or a commute, or nine hours of head-splitting boredom, Lucas was lost.

It was as if he had never experienced a weekend, and found the prospect a terror.

His heart began to race. The room was suddenly too small. His chest felt heavy, as if someone was sitting on it. Sweat pricked his brow and he became certain, somehow, that he was going to die.

So Lucas went outside. The world was, at last, big enough to breathe. He sat in the sun, still feeling the nightmare, and waited with clenched fists. He sat until things returned to normal … except that now, "normal" included a quiet horror that whatever had just happened could easily happen again.

He drew a deep breath and reassured himself out loud. "It's fine. I'm fine."

The moment passed, but the disquiet went nowhere.

Shelby usually slept in, but it felt right to wake her. They should maybe go to the zoo. Or out to breakfast. They could watch TV — anything, really, except for the stillness. Silence right now was a little too loud.

He sat on the couch, then stood and looked back at it. For a blip he could see someone else lounging upon the cushions.

Someone slumped.

Someone sleepy.

Without help, he dragged the couch to the French doors off of the patio. Its feet on wood made an unholy squealing, enough that Shelby made a show of plugging her ears. Once off the porch, Lucas dragged it across the lawn, to the side gate, and finally out front to the curb. He had no idea if the garbagemen would take a couch, but anywhere was better than inside the house.

Shelby was sitting in the La-Z-Boy and watching him with big round eyes when he returned. The room seemed empty with just the chair and a coffee table.

"Let's get a new one," he said.

The furniture store made him feel better. The place was full of customers — almost obnoxiously so. The space was big and bright. Lucas couldn't really afford a new couch, even once Kate's life insurance kicked in. But it wasn't like he could just keep staring at the old one.

They were loading the sofa when Miranda, emerging from the market next door, came over to greet them.

"Hi." Lucas gave her a nod.

"Shopping?"

For some reason he didn't want to tell her. Unfortunately, Shelby had no such qualms. She pointed at two men carrying a plastic-wrapped couch through the front door and into his beat-to-hell pickup, idling at the curb with its flashers on.

"We got a new couch," he said.

Miranda was studying Lucas's face, weighing his action, preparing to butt in and order him around. But then she reached into her pocket and pulled out a quarter. "Shelby, honey. Why don't you pick out a gumball?"

The girl looked back at a six-foot-tall machine — half dispenser, half barber pole. An elaborate mousetrap of domino actions filled its insides, making *getting* the candy as fun as having it in the end.

"Gumballs?" Lucas said as the girl walked away. "She's six."

"That's old enough for gumballs."

"You really are her mother now, aren't you?"

There was silence for a long time. Lucas was determined not to break it.

Miranda checked Shelby, saw that her gumball was still making its way through the contraption, then turned back to Lucas. "I'm worried about you."

"I thought I was a coward. Cowards run. They have nothing to be afraid of."

"Are you sleeping? You look terrible."

"Thanks. You too, Miranda."

"Can I come over?"

"For sex?"

This, finally, was too much. "Jesus, Lucas. What's happened to you? You were never this crude."

A flash of something returned to Lucas from his dream. It felt familiar even though it wasn't. Like déjà vu.

"Let me come over for a while. I'll even cook, if you want me to."

"Kinky."

"You know what?" Miranda shook her head. "Fuck you."

Shelby returned with her gumball to find the adults trading a stare. Then, maybe because it pissed Lucas off, she took Miranda by the hand. "Miss Miranda? Are you coming over today?"

"I don't know, honey …"

Shelby tugged her arm, just shy of swinging from it. "*Pleeeeease?* Can you come over, then you and me and Daddy can all play a game?"

Miranda silently turned the question to Lucas.

"Will you help carry the couch?" he asked her.

"Of course. I'll help with anything I can."

"I don't need help with anything else."

Miranda seemed to war with saying one thing before choosing another. "I'll help you with the couch, if you'll agree to consider something."

Lucas nodded slowly. She always told him what to do, so what was the difference now? Besides, she owed him. A lot of fault had gone into him needing a new couch in the first place, and at least some of it was hers.

"I want you to remember that you can't isolate your way out of pain," Miranda said when he seemed to nonverbally reply. "Remember, Lucas, that no man is an island."

THE GAME, called *Lords of the Atoll,* was a simplified version of *Dungeons and Dragons* with a hint of *Risk,* both of which Lucas had played as a kid. There were dice and hit points, but attributes like charisma were discarded, with the affair tailored to children as young as eight. Shelby had been in love with the game for a full year — since she was barely five. Not surprising. She'd been born precocious, reading as much as she played with her dolls or built with her Erector set.

Instead of expanding to include lesser beings, *Lords* cut to the top. Every player was royalty, either a king or a queen. You weren't a multitude, but the lore implied that you commanded one. Players warred king to king, attempting to overthrow one another until only one remained — no armies required.

Miranda kept sneaking looks at Lucas as they played. He pretended not to see them, but quickly grew preoccupied, knowing what she was thinking: Neither of them was sure whether they'd broken up. Their argument on Monday was a little knock-down-drag-out with no conclusion. They'd ended with a few jabs, and a request. Miranda still wanted to discuss that thing he really didn't want to talk about at all.

She rolled both dice, came up doubles.

"You're back to full strength!" Shelby declared.

Miranda was confused. "I am?"

"You rolled doubles."

Miranda had read the instructions before starting, but reached for them again now.

Lucas spoke to stop her. "It's a house rule."

"A 'house rule'?"

"Yeah. Like how in Monopoly, some people put all the Community Chest and Chance money in the middle of the board, and whoever lands on Free Parking takes it."

Miranda looked at her game piece, then her score sheet. "But I'm practically dead."

Lucas sighed because he'd raised the same point often in the past.

"We get to play longer this way," Shelby explained.

"Doesn't that make it impossible to win?"

"Yes." Lucas nodded. "It does."

"It makes it impossible to *lose*," Shelby clarified. "Isn't that more fun?"

Miranda turned to Lucas, who was content to let the argument continue so long as Miranda didn't poke at it. He shrugged: *Whatcha gonna do?*

"Don't look at me. Talk to Shelby. I keep telling her, games don't have a point if there aren't any stakes. It always ends with two kings who can't die. Then it goes on. And on. *Forever*."

Miranda turned back to her. "Then how do you know when to stop?"

"When Mommy makes us, and then …" Shelby stopped, suddenly dour.

"Maybe we set a timer," Lucas suggested into the silence, "and play five more minutes."

MIRANDA WAS AT THE MANTEL, examining the snow globe.

The thing showed a palm tree on a green swatch of land, surrounded by water. As with all snow globes — shaking sent white flakes everywhere. Lucas said it was ridiculous to have snow on palm trees, but that was why Kate had to have it. She'd called it "our climate-change globe" — a joke inside enough to become family legend, and earn the tchotchke a permanent spot on the mantel.

Lucas felt okay now — no jitters, no defenses lined up to take Miranda down at the first signs of meddling. It had been hours since the market, and almost a full hour since the game finished. Shelby was drawing in her room. They had gone in to check on her a few minutes ago. Together. It felt like something a pair of parents would do. Miranda asked what she was making with her colored pencils, and Shelby said it was the game they had just played. She'd handed the paper to her father, who'd looked it over with a level of serene pride he hadn't felt for what seemed like years.

No drama. No fighting. No hurt feelings or accusations. Just two adults and a kid in the lamp-lit bedroom. There was a drawing of two men at a very long table, with a chandelier of candles overhead. Through a sketched window was the long rock line of a breakwater, barring waves from the ocean. An odd detail for a kid to imagine, but Shelby had always been wise for her age.

That was ten minutes ago. Now the living room felt like a ticking clock.

Miranda wouldn't stay silent. Her intuition was what had first attracted Lucas, back when their relationship was still so very wrong. She returned the snow globe to the mantel, then came over to sit beside Lucas on the new sofa.

"Interesting game you play."

"Shelby likes it."

"Do you?"

"Sure." Lucas shrugged. "But mostly I like that she likes it."

Miranda trailed her fingers across the couch. "Why does one character drive a Firebird?"

"What?"

"I figured they'd ride horses. Fight with swords."

"They do fight with swords."

"Right. So why the Trans Am?"

"There's no Trans Am."

"You said it when you made your big move toward the end. Remember?"

Lucas shook his head. Miranda seemed to drop it, again drawing lines with her fingers. "Didn't Chad drive a Trans Am?"

Lucas felt his jaw tighten. "What Chad?"

"You know what Chad."

More silence.

"What about the cabin?" Miranda asked.

"Cabin?"

"You kept calling the fortress in the game a 'cabin.'"

"No I didn't."

"You did."

"I've played that game a lot more than you have, Miranda."

"So you added a cabin? Like another house rule?"

"I didn't say anything about a cabin," Lucas replied, his discomfort percolating.

"Yes you did. You said it like ten times." Miranda looked toward the bedrooms. "We could ask Shelby."

Lucas turned to her with all those defenses decidedly raised, but they instantly withered at the sight of her turned-away profile. It sounded like she was picking at him, but her face displayed something else. Her eyes were soft and glistening. She subtly wiped one and her fingers came away wet.

Like a snap, Miranda's entire past hour made perfect sense to Lucas. There had been something off about her, and he assumed she'd been uncomfortable — maybe even afraid of him yelling at her again. With this new context, he now understood that she'd been holding something in, refusing to let it show. Now it was threatening to erupt. There was deep sadness right at the surface, but this time it wasn't about Kate. Miranda looked afraid, too. Fretting like a parent agonizing over their hospitalized child.

"What?" he said, instead of snapping at her.

She sniffed and finally turned toward him. "I'm worried about you."

"You said that before."

She made a *be-calm* gesture, clearly wary of triggering

yet another explosion. "Not about drinking or missing work or any of that. I know you're clean. I'm worried that you're …" Miranda stopped, fighting emotion, and shook her head as if to deny it all. "I think something's broken." She touched her head. "In here."

Lucas laughed, until she stopped him with her eyes.

"You don't hear yourself. You don't see it. Yesterday, you left work early. Where did you go?"

"Jesus, Miranda. I don't really feel like being—"

She held out a hand. "*Please.*"

"I needed some boards to fix the back fence. I went to Home Depot."

"Is the wood in your garage?"

"Yeah."

"Where?"

"Right in the middle. What's this about?"

"I came through the garage. You parked inside, I parked in the driveway."

"I know that."

"There's no wood in your garage, Lucas."

He squinted, then shook his head. "I mean, I already fixed it."

"The fence?"

He nodded.

"Can we go out back and see it?"

"What's this about, Miranda?"

Her tone changed. "That day, I left work early too … and I followed you."

"You—?"

But again she held out that hand. "Just listen. Please. I followed you because you've been so strange. Do you remember running into me at the West 13th gas station? The Sunoco?"

"When?"

"Last week."

"I didn't run into you at the Sunoco."

She sniffed harder, swiping at a tear as it fell. "*Yes, you did*. I was at the next pump while you were gassing your truck. I saw you and said, 'Hey stranger, how are you?' Just playing. But you … I could tell you didn't know who I was."

"That's ridiculous."

"I thought maybe you were high. I didn't think you'd take it very well if I told you not to drive under the influence. So I followed you instead. To a construction site. You walked through a few of the plastic-curtained rooms, then drove to Wayfair Lake."

Lucas made himself laugh. "That's just …"

"You stood by the lake for most of an hour. Right at the water's edge. Looking down at the ripples. For an *hour*, Lucas!"

"Maybe I *was* high."

"So on the day you left work early, I followed you again. This time I took pictures."

"Okay, enough kidding around."

"You went to the quarry. Lucas, I … I thought you were going to jump!"

"Oh, bullshit."

"*Look! Look* if you don't believe me!" Miranda grabbed her phone and started tapping its surface.

Lucas stood and walked to the room's other side, waving the device away.

"I think you're having some sort of a breakdown," she said, fighting to keep from losing what little still remained of her control. "You're missing things. Confusing things. You kept doing it through the entire game, and never even noticed!"

"Freudian slip," Lucas muttered. "I've had a lot on my

mind."

"Yes! Yes you have!" Her tears spilled freely now. "You're trying to deal with this alone, but it's poisoning you inside! You talk in your sleep. Just the other night you said something about—"

"Stop."

"Lucas, listen to me!"

"STOP!" He shot a glance at the bedroom hallway. Then he took Miranda by the arm, dragged her into his office, and shut the door. "Keep your voice down. You're going to scare her."

A disbelieving expression stole over her face. Miranda laughed but the sound was bitter like cacao and ashes. "She's *already* scared! Lucas, for Christ's sake, the girl lost her mother! The woman she always looked to as her model for womanhood sat right there on your old couch and swallowed an entire vial of pills!"

Now Lucas was furious: papa bear mode. He didn't know what crap Miranda had gotten into her head, but she was reciting horrors he was already far too familiar with. "I know what she *fucking did.* Shelby found her, too. You know that?"

"Of course I know that! But did you ever *talk* to her about it? Or did you just let a six-year-old invent whatever story she wanted? *'Mommy wasn't happy. Mommy wanted to get away from me.'* You know kids blame themselves for suicides, don't you?"

"Shelby knows who's to blame."

"Does she, Lucas? Or is that a story you're telling yourself?"

"Oh, for fuck's sake. I thought we were past this."

"We never even got into it! Who *is* to blame, in your version of events? What do you tell yourself, Lucas, to avoid the truth?"

"I SAID THAT'S ENOUGH!"

She held herself taut for a long moment, like she might attack with a flurry of fists. Then her balloon seemed to pop and Miranda started sobbing into her hands.

Lucas spied the new presence at the doorway.

It was Shelby, her face devastated, the snow globe about to fall from her hands.

Chapter Nineteen

THE WEATHER GREW TURBULENT, as if to thwart Atticus's plans and Gerd's intention to oppose them. Storms blew in out of nowhere, then settled over only the cabin like a cartoon cloud. Every time Atticus stepped outside, the wind whipped and lightning flashed, more often than not a branch was sundered from a tree to fall dangerously close to one of them — once almost crushing Atticus's Trans Am.

"Stop it," Atticus would say to Gerd, and Gerd had no idea how to respond.

Everything was different enough. Gerd didn't want things to change any more. He'd liked their old routine, arduous and frustrating though it may have been. Pointless and disgusting though it'd been. Meaningless, as it increasingly seemed, though it'd been. Comfort came from unchanging days: coffee for breakfast, a trip to the dock and the pit for one of them and Unwanteds to murder for the other, followed by an acrimonious dinner at night.

Sometimes it seemed that each of them had been put in place specifically to thwart the other, as if the whole thing was busywork to occupy them. But this had to be pointless.

Were they protecting *anything?* Were they the keepers of anything?

Or was it all a lie?

Now there were no trips to the pit. The weather seemed to feel that given any slack at all, the island-keepers might flee. The Authority must know of Atticus's plan to abandon this place and his duties. So for days on end nobody traveled south to the dock or north to the pit. More and more, there was no need. From the second-floor windows, they could see quite plainly that the pit was coming to them.

Long, red lines in the bedrock. Steam wafted out in scalding clouds when it rained. At times that steam was like fog, and impossible to see through. There may as well have been no more island. Only the cabin, and them all alone.

Atticus spoke again, as if Gerd hadn't heard him. "I said stop it. *Enough.*"

Gerd looked over. "It's not me who does this."

Atticus looked betrayed. Lied to. "*Of course* it's you. Stop the storms and release me. I am not here to oppose you. So do not oppose me."

"I don't know what you're talking about!"

Atticus huffed off and left Gerd baffled.

He stayed by the window for a while longer, watching the fissures spread. Their progress was visible. The pit's many tendrils were surrounding their fortress like nooses.

The girl came over and again she wrapped her arms around him. He'd opened floodgates by allowing it the first time. Now she hugged Gerd whenever she possibly could.

"Get off," he said, and nudged her halfheartedly.

"I want to let go."

"Then let go."

"You first."

"I'm not holding on."

The girl said nothing and released him. Now there were two sets of eyes back on the storm and the unrelenting fissures.

"Why do you come to me? You belong to Atticus. He's the one who found you. He's the one who 'Wanted' you."

It was cruel, and he knew it, but that was okay because she was a *thing*, not a *person*. Still, more and more Gerd had been using her name. Assuming she might even have feelings.

Shelby did not seem offended. "You both found me."

"Atticus found you."

"You both found me," she repeated.

Gerd relented first. There was no point in arguing with a child.

"I'm supposed to remind you of something, Daddy Gerd. I think maybe that's why I'm here."

"Remind me of what?"

"Of how it all began."

Gerd felt watched. Someone had put her up to this. He glanced back over his shoulder. "Who told you to tell me anything?"

"You did."

"No I didn't."

"Yes, you did."

Gerd watched the storm. Atticus had attempted escape several times, but something always shoved him right back. "Atticus told me yesterday that he thinks the island has no western edge."

"You're avoiding what I wish to talk about."

"Because I don't want to——"

The sounds of wind and deluge first interrupted Gerd, then filled the silence between them.

"I'm supposed to remind you," Shelby began, "that you are not alone."

"Obviously."

"You act as if you know," she said.

"Clearly I know."

"How?"

"Because you are here. And Atticus is here. He is the constant thorn in my side."

"Have you ever wondered *why* he's here? Why Atticus exists?"

Gerd laughed. "That's one for the philosophers."

"Why do you collect only black and white stones?"

"What?"

"You never allowed yourself any colors."

"Atticus decides my stones."

"And still you don't wonder why he's here?"

Gerd walked away.

The girl followed. "We're still talking."

"*You're* talking. I'm going to my quarters."

"If Atticus gave you colored demand stones, would you have used them?"

"I use what I'm given."

"Yes. You do. You're very reliable that way, Daddy. You accept whatever you wish to see."

"Christ," Gerd said, doubling his speed.

"What am I to you?" asked the girl, running now.

"A pest."

"Then what is Atticus?"

"Also a pest. The both of you are obstacles."

"The pit isn't spreading, you know. It's always covered the island, from end to end. Only now it's dying … it's finally showing itself."

He put a door between them, and slammed it, clearly on his side of the cabin.

"Daddy Gerd?" the door seemed to say.

"Go away. I'm through with this."

Something strange happened. For a moment, the girl-thing's voice matured, sounding like someone much older. It bellowed in fury,

"WE NEVER EVEN GOT INTO IT!"

Gerd blinked. The room didn't want to stay in focus.

A vision intruded instead.

He saw a woman, on a couch, slumped with one hand hanging over the arm. An image from a horrible nightmare of something that had been done to him. It was the conspiring of many, yet in the dream Gerd paid the price.

He opened the door. The girl was still there, looking expectantly up at him. She held a glass bauble: a tree on a tiny island, covered in snowflakes.

His mind went fuzzy. Gerd hadn't wanted to hear what Shelby had to say at all. But now the opposite was true. He found himself falling into something like a trance. Wanting to know. *Needing* to know.

"What's happening?" Gerd asked as the hypnotic haze spread into every corner of the room.

"You're not alone," she told him. "But alone is how it began."

AND SO THE GIRL, now that she had Gerd's attention, said:

"At first there was only you. There was no cabin, no waves, no sea. No island. No docks, no pit, no creatures, no vehicles and no roads on which to drive them. At first there was only the map, drawn on blank paper. One player alone, with no troubles or worries, and all the world's power. Do you remember?"

Gerd remembered.

"Of course you were immortal. Of course you were omnipotent and omniscient, as far as the rules went. You were a politician who wins a race because he's run uncontested. You were the only draw in a lottery. If there had been any arguments, you'd have won every one.

"Then one day the island came. First the land and water, then the pit. It promised a departure from boredom, meaning in the absence of nothing. Everything around you seemed to come from nowhere, but you know where it came from now, don't you?"

Gerd blinked. His gaze fell on that glass dome with a palm tree inside.

And yes, he knew it now.

"At first the island had no purpose, so writing was all there was. It occupied you, and gave you comfort in your isolation. But you could not allow such a thing — so as your thoughts focused, you spawned new things from that interior place of imagination and creation, without even knowing it. One day you went south and there was a set of pillars in the water that hadn't been there before. Lines ran from the tops into the deep. Back then it was only ten feet, maybe less. At the north was a shallow mine. You walked the island and found the lobster traps right where you expected them. You walked the mine. And the paths. You stayed east, never bothering to go west, because by then the place was its own story.

"As stories always do, this one wrote itself inside you. So you transcribed the tale of this place and said, *'Maybe the pit is this. Maybe this is what I do.'* It became those things, and you forgot about before. It was safer that way, because islands must come from someplace. In time the forgetting held more reality than truth, and on that day the island had suddenly always existed. Eternal rather than you. Do you remember?"

Gerd remembered.

"The island tried to tell you something. When you didn't like its message, Atticus arrived. But you knew those sorts of things don't happen, so to believe they had to put the island in a specific box, precisely where you did not want it. So you let the island be real. And Atticus could live here forever. At first he agreed with all that you said. But then he began to explore. To build. To wonder. To *ask*. He became a villain — a yin to your yang. It never exactly *happened*. It was simply forever ago.

"I came next. To him, but also to you. At first I was nothing. Like early Atticus, I believed the story you told. But look at me now, Daddy Gerd. Am I new? Or have you already told yourself that it's always been the three of us on this island? Forever and ever? For thousands of years? Since the dawn of time? Is that how it is?"

Shelby was as she'd been for thousands of years: always here, always on Atticus's infuriating side, always around to tell Gerd that he was getting it wrong.

"Do you remember why you came here, Daddy?" She put the snow globe into his waiting hands. "Do you remember now?"

The globe. The Unwanted. The tedium of it all, and the non-time, non-space of this place.

Yes. Now he remembered.

Chapter Twenty

There was nothing at all.

No cabin. No island. No house, no mantel holding a snow globe. No new couch, no old couch. No weapons, no vehicles, no dice or hit points.

No Miranda. No Atticus.

There was only Gerd. And Lucas. And the girl.

He was alone on one side of a sparse white void. Lucas and Shelby occupied the other, both waiting for him to speak.

Emotion came. Gerd shook his head, refusing to look at them. One felt like staring at the present and the other like peering right into the future's eyes.

But it was the past, unrepresented by either, that dogged them. The past they'd come here to witness.

"No," Gerd said. "I can't."

"You can."

"I won't." His breath tried to hitch. His heart was trapped in his throat.

"You have to," said the man who looked just like him, "or more we shall suffer."

The girl seemed smaller than before, her face devastated. A pigeon in front of a hammer's blow, eyes pleading for the bully to spare her.

But in addition to Gerd

(Lucas)

and the girl, he now remembered quite clearly that there had also been a woman. Someone to turn this father-and-daughter pairing into a family of three.

He'd shut that woman in a closet, disavowed, forcing himself to forget her forever.

The three of us, on vacation. On an island. Hawaii, where there was no snow. She shook it and said, "This one's climate change." They'd laughed. And loved. Before the trouble, in the honeymoon after Old Gerd and Old Lucas had gone away and New Gerd, New Lucas, had taken their place.

For a while.

Until the creature, like Atticus, had risen inside him.

But no …

He would not let it start that way. Not with another lie.

And so he corrected himself: *No creature rose inside me. I called it forth, willingly and shamefully, from deep within myself. And that was how the ruin began.*

One happy family, obliterated by a careless hand.

At this thought — this admission — Lucas moved to Gerd's side of the void, took his hand, and did something extraordinary.

The men … *merged* somehow.

Two people were suddenly one.

And then it was just Lucas and Shelby. Father and daughter in the strange white void.

A little girl waiting for her daddy to tell a story that he'd never told before.

"Okay." Lucas swallowed. "This is how it begins."

Chapter Twenty-One

NOT LONG AGO, *in a land close to home, a prince and princess and their daughter lived in a small but handsome castle, on a quiet suburban street of edged lawns and tidy bushes. White fences crawled from yard to yard. It was a lovely life, and in it, the family was happy.*

Princess Kate was clever, smart, and lovely. A genius with those she knew, always quick to make friends. She was generous, and so very kind.

The prince was talented and creative, spending his days in an office and his evenings smithing words. He told stories that served him, that painted the world as he saw it instead of how it was. At first, that didn't matter. Later, it did.

The prince and princess were perfect. Until one day, a stranger arrived.

The stranger was new to the land. She worked at a coffee shop the prince visited daily and she liked him very much. She flirted. He flirted. It came easily.

Before Princess Kate, Prince Lucas had enjoyed the companionship of many ladies. That was supposed to be in the past, but he'd unsuccessfully caged his urges, without them ever really going away.

The prince was a master of disguise, a wizard of sorts. He had the power to bewitch suitors and was gifted at lying right to the princess's face.

And so it came to be that two or three days a week, the prince fucked the stranger wherever, whenever, and however he could. When it ended, he found a different lady of the court and fucked her, too.

After, he went home. He took a shower, told an untrue story, and ate dinner as if nothing had happened.

But the princess was far more clever than the prince believed, and in no way fooled. She confronted the prince. He lied very, very well, but even as she halfway believed his deceptions, a deeper part of herself did not believe them at all.

The princess started to tell another story to herself…

That the prince was dutiful but weak, that he couldn't help himself, that he wasn't actually doing those things anyway (though she knew he was), and ultimately that he remained a good father and she still somehow loved him.

She turned to a potion-maker, who offered her square pills with a K-shape cut in the middle. Her pills reduced stress. Reduced anxiety. Made her better able to believe both the prince's lies, and those she told herself.

Then one day, a second stranger arrived — this one named Chad, arriving on a Trans Am chariot.

He met the prince first, and the two became fast friends. They had so much in common. The stranger complimented the prince's stories. His words flattered the prince, and the prince, being only a man, grew fond of his flattery. The stranger brought introductions to the right people. He even helped the prince sell his stories on the internet. And so the stranger flourished one hand to bewitch the prince, while his other worked elsewhere. Specifically, under the princess's skirt.

But carnality was only the cutting edge of what ran between them. The stranger was kind to the princess when the prince was absent. He sat with the princess and listened to her, interested in what she had to say. The stranger made the princess feel valuable, and interesting, and attractive — all things the prince seemed to have forgotten while he was getting his pole waxed by trashy baristas.

Because the stranger, you see, wasn't really a predator. He wasn't actually a wolf who came dressed in sheep's clothing. He was simply there when the princess needed him and the prince was off putting his dick in someone else. He did not urge her into anything. What happened between them came naturally.

But unlike with the prince, the princess's infidelity tore at her soul. She felt better with the stranger, and far worse without him. The prince still came home and told his lies, and her temptation to believe them only deepened her depression.

For the princess, unbeknownst fully to anyone but herself, had carried a wound since her abjectly shitty teen years: a certainty that she would never be good enough — not for the prince, not for the stranger, not for her co-workers, not for anyone who depended on her.

As the sad circumstances continued — and as she popped more and more Klonopin to smother her sorrow and troubles over Prince Cock's philandering, the princess became convinced she was worthless in one other way: as a mother. How could she pretend at a happy family while the prince was bending over his ladies in waiting and she, knowing it, did nothing but cheated right back?

All the while, the prince kept bringing Stranger Chad around, unaware that he was being cuckolded, seeing the uncomfortable and confusing looks on her face when they all had dinners together and dismissing them as more of her infuriating mood swings.

And so it went, for three long months.

But the prince was not, as is popularly believed, distraught. He'd been taken in by dark magic, and he called the rapturous sorcery "pussy." The magic made him unwise. And forgetful of all he had. It made him cruel and uncaring. In the old language, it made the prince a staggeringly horseshit-faced asshole, willfully blind.

Yet, at the same time, as if the prince were a fucking psychopath or sociopath or whatever-the-hell term it is, he also managed to feel bad for himself. He suspected the princess was up to something, but somehow it was more her fault than his.

He told himself that he was innocent.

He blamed whichever man was comforting her — maybe even bedding her.

He blamed her medications, which had expanded from anti-anxiety drugs to a medicine cabinet full of antidepressants.

The blame justified his own sleeping around — because why should he stay home with someone so boring and whiny?

But our sad story has yet to hit its lowest point.

One day, Stranger Chad caught a bit of conscience like a common cold. Unasked, he came to the prince and told him of his affair, informing the prince that he'd already ended things, if only for young Princess Shelby's sake, because he couldn't be the one to break up a family.

The prince punched Chad hard enough to break his teeth, then went to sleep with Maid Miranda. The prince had set the stage with Maid Miranda, who'd been a friend of the princess's since college, by telling her that he and the princess were divorcing.

There was no adultery, he said; they'd already broken up. These, like many of the prince's lies, weren't really deceptions inside his mind. The prince believed he was divorcing. He just didn't bother to tell Maid Miranda that he was causing the split — and Miranda, wooed but unable to face the princess, had not the knowledge to contradict him.

Princess Kate, meanwhile, was left alone. Left with all that hideous darkness now exposed inside her. She had no one to tell her she was clever. No one to tell her she was beautiful. No one to tell her she had value.

And so she came to disbelieve all of those things. The princess, who'd once lit the neighborhood with her smile, found herself worthless and alone. So she looked long and hard at the warnings on her Klonopin vial, then sat on the living room couch and downed the entire thing with a poisonous amount of vodka.

The prince claimed to be on a business trip that night. Young Princess Shelby was staying with a friend, due to return midday, after the prince's return.

But the prince did not return on time and Shelby came early, entering the unlocked home as her friend's mother's car drove away. She knew to call 911, but it was already too late.

And so the story ends: in sorrow. For there could have been a lesson to this tale, but it went unnoticed.

The prince, who still cared very much for the princess despite the wanderings of his wayward appendage, was devastated. The pain was more intense than anything he'd ever felt before. In the height of that agony, the prince knew exactly who'd caused this tragedy. He himself had cast every stone.

But the pain was crippling enough to literally turn off the world.

The prince could not continue to exist. Or look into the mirror without wanting himself murdered.

He could not comfort Miranda, who'd lost a friend, whose own guilt was fathoms deep, who thought she'd been involved with a separated man, not a fully married one.

But most of all, he could not face his daughter.

The girl favored her mother, and in Shelby, the prince saw Kate. Every glance at her was a hard stare at the princess's dead body.

The princess, sprawled out on the couch with one hand dangling and vomit crusted on her chin.

A vision he couldn't stop seeing in his dreams because he'd been too absent to see it in life.

But at the same time, the prince clung to young Shelby, needing to protect the last of his family. To save her, because he could not save himself.

So in order to get past the pain, the prince had to forget.

In order to do what he could, he had to change the past. He could not be a father and a negligent murderer at the same time. He could not be a role model, staring into the eyes of a girl whose mother he'd driven to suicide.

There was only one way to change the past, and that was to tell himself a story.

And the story went:

A long time ago, in a land far away, a prince and princess lived in a large and awe-inspiring castle …

Chapter Twenty-Two

SᴏMETHING very heavy struck Gerd in his shoulder.

At first he thought it was a club, but it turned out to be something between a broadsword and a handheld guillotine: a huge steel weapon it should have by rights taken two people to swing. But Atticus managed to bury the blade six inches into the muscle between Gerd's shoulder and neck just fine by himself.

The pain was exquisite. Quite literally like nothing Gerd had ever experienced. He could feel the blade's breadth opening him like a seasoning slit in a roast. His head lolled, tendons severed, and his head felt eaten by flames. Blood poured in a river. Somehow even his plasma hurt. The blow weakened his knees, so as he collapsed in agony, his shins hurt from impact. His hands, which slapped the bloodied deck, were an extra rimshot of pain as he fell upon them.

His deeper injury was psychic. The bodily pain was intense, but the agony he felt outside himself was ten times as strong. The suffering was existential: a desperate, hopeless sort of pain that would never, ever end.

Atticus wrenched the blade from Gerd like a cleaver from a ham hock, now above him while Gerd tried to find his bearings. He stood with the weapon hanging at his side. Shelby was still where she'd been, now not far from Atticus. Her expression was, ironically, so much more accusing than it'd been before he'd retold his story.

"You son of a bitch," Atticus said.

But something was strange. Atticus was grimacing. His own shoulder sagged, and despite the devastating blow he'd landed on Gerd, he appeared to be the injured one.

Gerd reached into the pain. It was nearly impossible. His wound was already stitching, though, so he raised his hips and shot both feet like pistons into the other man's groin.

Atticus staggered back, grabbing his jewels, but at the same time the kick drained Gerd of his waning strength. Now his whole middle hurt, as if the hatchet wound had spread southward.

The lights flickered, then died. A storm was suddenly raging, lightning turning the upstairs space into a photo strobe. But something else was even stranger.

They were in Gerd's rooms. How had Atticus gotten inside?

Gerd pushed himself upward, pain still a swinging anvil above him. There was a lamp on a nearby bookcase with a heavy iron base. Gerd picked it up, inverted it, then swung it to shatter Atticus's jaw.

More pain — strange this time because he hadn't been hit. Gerd tightened his grip to strike Atticus again … and again … and again, fighting new agony each time. After fifteen swings or more, Atticus was unrecognizable even in long strikes of lightning. His face looked inside out. More a pile of bloody offal at the end of his neck than a head.

Panting, heaving, Gerd tossed the lamp aside. It made

a sound like a tank shell when striking the wooden floor. Then he slumped onto his rear and one hand, crippled as if he'd taken the beating.

Deep, full-body sighs took him. He'd literally never felt worse in his life.

Then a jolt of brand-new pain, this time at the back of his neck. He became aware of something odd in his mouth, then closed his teeth to find the cutting edge of a blade between them. His eyes tried to look back but his head would not turn.

"Don't you get it, you stupid piece of shit?" Atticus grated from behind him, twisting the speared knife through his brain stem. "Even now, *do you still not see?*"

Gerd spun them both, the momentum whipping Atticus and his knife free.

Atticus hit the wall, his face already mostly healed. Gerd's shoulder wound had stitched, his slashed shirt hanging like a tattered drape. He could still feel the hole through the back of his neck with his tongue.

Atticus roused, then stood like a fighter. Gerd took one look at Shelby, still just watching, and ran down the stairs like a coward.

A helmet from a suit of armor slammed him in the skull halfway down, thrown by Atticus.

Atticus sprinted toward Gerd as Gerd lost balance and fell. The stab through the cerebellum hadn't helped his coordination any; he'd been barely getting his legs to work as it was. His heart hadn't really returned to beating yet and his lungs weren't working, but it was his failure to soften the fall that mattered most.

In vertigo, Gerd lost track of the stone steps until he'd half-spun, fell hard, and slammed head-first into them. His skull opened in the same spot the helmet had struck. There was a sensation of wetness, then a mental fog and a slippery, gel-like sensation beneath him. It seemed he was sliding down the steps via the lubrication of his own brain.

The indignity didn't stop there. The steps were steep, wide, and long, and as Atticus skittered down behind him, Gerd's body continued to flee. He rolled, flipped end-over-end, and finally struck the anteroom floor with every limb broken.

Atticus was over him holding an enormous sphere: an Atlas stone turned from decoration to weapon.

He swung. Gerd, wiggling more than crawling, curled inside the downward arc and came up between Atticus's legs just as the stone struck floor. He did the predictable thing, uppercutting Atticus's testicles with all the might of his healing arm.

Second shot to the nuts in three minutes. Gerd, old boy, you're not fighting fair.

Atticus tottered; Gerd lunged for a shotgun mounted on the wall beneath the dueling pistols, eternally loaded with at least three shells. He unloaded them one after another into Atticus: head, chest, gut.

Half of Atticus painted the floor and wall behind him while the rest remained temporarily upright, eventually collapsing like a pile of rags.

Gerd sprinted for the front door. His body was whole again, but the pain had yet to depart. He felt punched in the nuts. He felt like he'd been shot in the head, chest, and gut. But most of all he felt that same existential dread: an agony that existed in some sort of astral body. Pain stuffed his mouth full of cloth, forcing him to gasp rather than breathe. Pain smashed his heart into paste, and yet it still tried to beat.

Gerd wrenched the door open to find Atticus on the stoop, drenched in rain. There was no more land outside. No more breakwater, no more ocean. The grounds were laced with steaming red fissures, the pit opening beneath them. Atticus grabbed Gerd by the throat as he gaped.

"I'm not behind you. Get it?" Atticus shouted above the wind and whoop of the storm. *"I'm not in front of you. Get it?"*

Gerd croaked, "What the hell are you tal—?"

But Atticus had grown impossibly strong. He shoved him back into the foyer and then, using just his throttling hand, Atticus swung Gerd against the wall like a chambermaid beating a rug. The stone cracked in an oblong web behind him.

Then he let go and Gerd, concussed and bleeding anew, tried to look up. He'd left the door open. A fierce rain was blowing into the anteroom, coming in sheets. Shadows danced in staccato lighting. At first there was only dim, then the whole world became light … over and over against the soundtrack of oblivion.

"You can't kill me; don't you understand? The game *itself* is your hell … and it goes on forever!"

Gerd swept Atticus's leg, shoving his own leg between the angle of floor and calf as Atticus fell. The inserted limb became a fulcrum; Atticus's own weight snapped first calf, then femur. White bone pierced his pants and skin. Atticus wailed.

Gerd wasted no time. He rushed into the storm, fighting to see through driving rain, fighting to remain on his feet. What was left of the soil around the cabin had become inky mud. He could see no more than twenty feet out. The cars were nowhere in sight. The rock shifted underfoot and he staggered back as a new piece of ground fell away, rotating lazily into the pool of lava bubbling up from the bottom.

Then Atticus was atop him again. Gerd rolled fast and did the most primitive thing, hitting him in the face as he lay on the dirt. But it seemed that Gerd, too, had gained new strength, because his first blow collapsed his enemy's head like an apple-face doll. Atticus was suddenly concave.

So Gerd hit him again, and again, and again, just with his fist now, until Atticus's neck was bent back and his head had been punched into the ground like the first tissue through the top of a tissue box.

He was soaked. Lost. He'd forgotten where he was. Staring into the unending downpour was vertigo; the horrible sensation that still hadn't left him was a too-large fist gripping every one of his internal organs.

What *was* this place? It wasn't an island; that much was sure. It seemed to be a Hell pit with a cabin on top as some sort of wiseass decoration. But it wasn't a small suburban home, either, and Gerd seemed to remember getting a new couch that was nowhere in sight, and he remembered a quarry, a pit, a lake, an ocean. He remembered a woman somewhere who still managed to like him, even though he was shit on the shoe of a syphilitic traveler.

Then Atticus had him by the neck, behind him in a headlock, his weight now massive. He pushed Gerd toward one of the boiling lava vents and held him in the scalding steam, blistering his face.

"You don't deserve to live! I don't deserve to live!" Atticus shook him, still holding tight as if trying to break his neck. The scalding steam was impossibly cruel. Gerd felt his face seem to melt and slide off.

"You want redemption? We don't *deserve* redemption!" The fissure cracked wider, and a much closer floe of hot rock revealed itself.

Atticus shoved him toward it.

Gerd rolled again, singeing Atticus's arm. Atticus hissed in pain and withdrew, and seconds later Gerd was back inside the cabin. But what was the point? In, out, in, out … There was no way to escape. No way to leave. No way to win.

There was only an eternal way to lose.

Shelby was in the room's center now, near the door to the dining room. The long black table with its candle chandelier swung in the door's breeze behind her.

"You have to help me," Gerd told the girl.

"Why should I help you?"

"I was wrong. *Shelby*. You have to believe me! I'm sorry for all I did. I'm sorry for—!"

Atticus reared in front of him, holding a morning star. Gerd tried to duck, but the metal smashed his skull and the points shredded him into bacon.

Then Atticus was over him again, but he wouldn't be unseated so easily this time; he was learning every second. Gerd tried to roll but he'd broadened himself, becoming impossible to flip. Again he tried for the testicles, but Atticus had protected them. Gerd couldn't move. Atticus's working face and hot, ugly breath filled his vision — clearer by the moment as life returned to him.

"I'm *you*," Atticus snarled at him. "You're *me*. Do you get it now? You aren't in prison. You don't get to serve your time and get back to your life. This isn't a sentence you have to pay. This is your Hell. Your eternity."

Gerd struggled and made no headway. Atticus laughed.

"Please," Gerd said.

"Tell it to Kate."

"I didn't know! I didn't know! And it was *you! You* did it, too!"

Atticus leaned back. Gerd expected him to shift his weight enough to kick free, but instead he reversed his trajectory and slammed his forehead into the bridge of Gerd's nose.

"What hurts you hurts me," Atticus said, his scalp

bleeding, dripping onto Gerd's shattered face. "What hurts Shelby hurts me. What hurts Kate and Miranda hurts me."

Then he delivered another head-butt, this time much harder.

"YOU KILLED HER! YOU SON OF A BITCH, WE KILLED HER!"

"It wasn't just us!"

"Jesus," Atticus said, furious and long-suffering.

"Cut his throat," Shelby said, handing him a silver fillet knife Gerd had last seen in the kitchen. Atticus rolled off, but instead of coming after Gerd with the blade, he held it to his own throat.

"This will hurt you," Atticus said, "exactly as much as it hurts me."

He dragged the knife across his throat. It slit halfway around, severing carotid, jugular, and windpipe in one deep slash. Gerd choked and shot his hand to his neck, tongue out and gagging as Atticus murdered himself.

But Atticus wasn't done. Confused and incapacitated, Gerd stumbled toward him. Atticus, gagging in the exact same way, simply stepped backward. He took the knife and slid it upward through his own voice box, ascending the trachea like exhaled breath.

A quick slash. Something dropped to the floor at the exact same moment a bolt of agony weakened Gerd's legs. He fell next to the dropped thing, then saw it was Atticus's tongue, cut free from the inside.

Ten seconds. The pain dimmed but remained enormous. Then Atticus was back on top of him, behind him now, and using his still-forming tongue to whisper with blood-copper breath into Gerd's ear.

"Dow *speath*," he gummed. "*Dow* thee if doo can speath your lies."

Atticus stood. But before Gerd could stand to join him, something huge shot downward through his neck and into the stone floor below him. He could no longer move, pinned by Atticus's iron spear, held in place like a pithed frog.

Atticus lowered himself to sit cross-legged, sideways from Gerd's view, ten feet away. Soon all but the freshest wound had healed, yet without the spear gone, Gerd was going nowhere.

His larynx was still impaled. He couldn't say a single word. No truths, and certainly no more lies.

The storm was dwindling. It rained outside, but the furious thunder and unrelenting wind were gone.

"You cannot speak," Atticus said, "so perhaps you will finally listen."

Chapter Twenty-Three

It FELT like hours had passed.

Gerd should have adjusted to the feeling of being pinned to the floor by now, but it wasn't the kind of thing a man could get used to. If he was very, very still, his agony around the spear would abate … but paralysis brought its own aches and pains, so he'd shift a limb, or attempt to roll his midsection, only to have his agony scream again. He couldn't swallow. Drool ran out and pooled below his mouth.

Atticus came and went. He'd said nothing since the pithing. Gerd could hear him rattling about both around and above him, doing God knew what.

Now you'll listen. But so far he'd said nothing.

That's how it was until the creatures came.

The door was still open. Worse, the fissures outside had begun to enter the cabin, splitting walls and floors to reveal the depths below. Atticus had said that the entire island was collapsing into the pit. Now, it seemed he'd been right.

Gerd watched the demons come, horrified. For the past few turbulent days, he'd forgotten about their old duties: the stones, the Gatekeeper, the black seeds they took from the chests of creatures and incubated just long enough to kill them from existence. Now, those duties had — in a sideways way — returned. Only now, Gerd didn't have to get stones anymore, or visit the Gatekeeper to redeem them. The creatures, like the pit, now came to him.

They climbed from the depths as the fissures opened. At first they circled him, breathing sulfur breath and gnashing at him with razor teeth.

But soon their behavior started to change. Now they were lying on their backs, using sharp claws to open their own bodies. Ichor spilled like black blood. Seed pods emerged on their own.

It seemed the Unwanted no longer needed incubation or time to hatch. Instead they were born immediately, crawling across Gerd leaving tar trails like the slime of a snail.

"Good news," said a voice.

Gerd strained over the teeming black things covering his chest to see that Atticus had returned, sweeping an area clean of Unwanted and arranging himself beside Gerd with crossed legs.

"I've arranged for us to stay," Atticus continued. "Here. In the cabin. It'll be different than before, but hey. Beggars can't be choosers, am I right?"

Gerd tried to speak — to protest — but got only agony for his efforts.

"What?" Atticus looked around as if the source of Gerd's discomfort wasn't obvious. "The Unwanted? Well, yes, they'll stay here with us, too. One big happy family — all of them and us. It'll be fun. Like sleeping in a pile of roaches, with them skittering into your thoughts and leaving you nightmares. And yeah, yeah, I know what you're going to say. *We don't want them,* right? By definition, we don't *want* Unwanted."

Gerd made a sound. Atticus took it as agreement.

"Oh yes. I know they're not wanted, but with your obstinance out of the way, I also know now *why* we don't want them. It's hardly new information. I tried to tell you as much, but I couldn't spoon-feed you. You understand the nature of the thing already, don't you, Gerd? You had to learn it for yourself."

Atticus gave an odd chuckle that was almost amused.

"What irony. I can't tell you anything unless *you* are able to tell it to yourself — unless *you'll* actually acknowledge the truth of things that *you* already know. Which makes me wonder: *Why am I even here?* You're not well, Lucas. Your denial is so profound, you can't even listen when you're the one speaking. Or perhaps I have it backward. Maybe you can't listen *because* it's you who's speaking."

Atticus crawled a few lengths forward, squinting at Gerd as if studying him. Gerd tried to flail an arm, but Atticus was still out of reach.

"I know when you're trying to grab me," Atticus said, watching Gerd's impotent hand flap. "You'd know that if you'd open your eyes. I know what you know, the same as I feel your pain. Same as you feel mine. You've set yourself an impossible game, don't you see? You're trying to fool yourself. You make plans, but you cannot keep them secret from me. You're simply pitting one part of yourself against another. There's an Authority in your head somewhere, but you cannot see it. Instead you blame the Authority we already know. Just as you blamed Chad and Kate for her death."

Gerd gurgled, but Atticus answered as if he'd heard words.

"Oh, sure, Kate invited Chad into her bed and Chad went where she wanted him. But are you really that unseeing? Do you really think that's where this all started?"

He paused, squinting harder before retracting to his earlier position. "It was their fault, right? Her. Him. The pills. Her sense of inadequacy, and later her addiction. *That's* who's to blame." Atticus offered Gerd an amused shake of his head. "Your logic is so fucked up. And to think, I was supposed to be the better you."

Gerd jerked. Blood was flowing again, covering his cheeks and infiltrating his mouth. Again he tried to speak. A partial word this time, barely audible, clotted by discharge: *"Thorry."*

"Oh. *We're sorry. That* unfucks the women we cheated with. *That* unkills our wife. We've been sorry before. Again and again and again. She thought we'd changed, believed that we'd settled down and stopped sleeping around. But we just can't be *pinned down*, can we?" Atticus laughed. "Well. Except for you. You're plenty pinned."

Again Gerd tried to say he was sorry for how he'd been — with feeling this time.

"No." Atticus shook his head, having none of it. "I don't buy your bullshit regret. And if *I* don't buy it, then *you* don't either. And yet I know you're sincere because *I'm* sincere, and that means *we mean it even though we don't believe it.*"

A sarcastic expression of frustrated disbelief crossed his face before he continued. "Don't you see how crazy that is? If we were truly a *bad* person, that might be better. Evil at least knows what it is, while we remain clueless. We've created a world for ourselves, and in it we're gods. We're *immortal.* We can't be wrong and we can never die. *Gods*, Lucas. Isn't that a funny way to apologize?"

Hordes of dripping Unwanteds climbed over them both.

Gerd cringed away, but the movement only opened his wound, causing him to bellow around the spear.

Atticus had opened his palms as if to welcome the crawling horrors into his lap. They climbed over his legs, stinging him with their stingers and biting him with their teeth. They ascended his chest to his neck, encircling it as if to strangle.

"We didn't accept what happened," Atticus continued. "We didn't atone for anything. Instead this fantasy of ours celebrated our lack of fault, crowning us kings. Instead of facing the real world, we came here, where there were no lessons to learn. But I have to wonder: *What kind of fool would prefer this existence?* It's true that we can't die, but we also can't live. Maybe we're free to do as we wish, but we're not *free* at all. We say the Authority holds sway, but who *is* the Authority? Does he — does *she* — exist? Does he — *she* — tell us what to do in a way we must obey? Or is it merely another excuse?"

"You," Gerd managed to croak.

"Yes. *Me.* Our enemies are each other. Me against me. You against you. You conjured me to explain your errors, then saw my advice as blame and refused to hear me. We were our own mutual roadblocks. I controlled your life and you controlled mine, both all-powerful. Who *really* held you back? Was it Kate's 'neediness and whining'? Responsibility for Shelby? Or Miranda, who stays by you even now, knowing the truth? She never wanted to be the other woman. Your lie *turned her into one.* A powerful enough of a lie to ruin three other lives."

"Thad," Gerd gurgled. Fortunately no explanation was needed. He was getting the hang of this. Atticus could always fill in the blanks.

His adversary nodded, to show understanding rather than agreement, then said, "Chad was the flame, but *you* set the tinder. Without him, there would have been someone else. You should thank him. In the desperate days before Kate took her own life, Chad was all she had to soften the despair."

One of the Unwanted climbed into Gerd's mouth. Panic filled him; he had no way to expel the thing. He tried to huff but had no breath.

But then Atticus started to laugh at his antics, and Gerd quickly saw why.

Across the floor, some of the hatchlings were slitting open bits of exposed skin on Atticus's legs and climbing inside. Others were doing the same at his neck and arms. Gerd realized they were doing the exact same thing to him. He'd been in denial again, this time about something right in front of his face.

"It's like I said," Atticus told him. "I've arranged for us to stay here. You helped, of course, but it's not like you even knew. And it's not like you could stop me because in order to do that you'd have to accept … *certain truths*. Stopping me would require self-honesty and restraint. You fear control, Gerd, because you can't control yourself."

More of the Unwanted entered his body through long bloody slits. Gerd could feel them now; it was like being trapped in a burlap bag with hundreds of wriggling rats. He squealed. Tried to scream.

"Oh, I'm not punishing you," Atticus told him. "*We're* punishing *us*. You want to stop me? Go ahead. Stop us both."

He tried to focus, but his attention was everywhere, and mostly fixed on the evil squirming between skin and muscle.

Atticus, on the other hand, seemed to be enjoying this.

"I guess you can't stop us. And really, that's the best part. *We're* in control. Not me. Not you. *Us.* One can speak for both. But you? You just *can't speak*, can you?"

Gerd croaked.

Atticus continued. "I think that at first we wanted to stay here forever, but the writing was immediately on the wall when you gave the girl to me. We built a place where we could always rule, even if in acrimony, but your inner self just couldn't let it be. You wanted to stay *and* to go. To wake up *and* stay asleep. To apologize *and* repent without *admitting* or *feeling or knowing* that you'd even done anything wrong."

Atticus sighed and spread his hands. "So here we are. Approach, avoid. Push and shove. But a stalemate could never finish the job, so Shelby was the one thing that could possibly bring it all into focus. Force our stalemate in one direction or the other."

Atticus made a sweeping gesture, indicating the room full of tiny black phantoms. "And now, the Unwanted? The things this place insisted we unearth then destroy without claiming responsibility? Now, my friend and enemy, there is no more stalemate. *We lose.* And now, all our deadly secrets will eat us alive."

Gerd was losing himself to the panic — worse than any he had ever felt before, even after a thousand years on the island.

Or maybe it was a lot less time.

Maybe it was no time at all.

Because maybe — just maybe — he wasn't really here.

"It's for the best, really," Atticus went on in a lazy voice. "What value does Lucas Latham have in the outside world? In here, he's more than a king. But out there? Well. Out there, he's less than nothing. If you ask me, Lucas ..." He snickered. "If you ask me, *Gerd*, old pal? If you ask me, I say that Lucas … that son of a bitch … deserves to die."

Gerd, even in his current shitty situation, thought he could accept that. Because it was true. Everything Atticus had said was true, and Gerd knew it deep down. He and Atticus were different manifestations of the same troubled mind. And they always had been.

He was his own worst enemy.

He had stood in his own way. Been his own jailer and tormentor.

And whose fault was it?

Whose fault was *all of this*?

Why it was *his*, of course. He wouldn't be in this mind-made prison if he didn't feel he was worthless and terrible. He wouldn't even be *on* the damned island … if he himself didn't feel like this was the punishment he deserved.

If he chose to no longer consider himself infallible and immortal, he could allow himself to die.

And so he decided.

But then Shelby caught his eye. She was far behind Atticus, standing by the doorway. She hadn't been there earlier, probably because none of this existed.

So *why* was Shelby here — now, then, or ever?

The only answer was himself. *He'd* brought her here. He'd dragged her into his Hell the same as he'd dragged Atticus: *for a reason.*

To remind him of his misdeeds.

Or maybe because deep down, he still wanted to save a life.

Not his.

Hers.

Atticus's face changed. Then quite suddenly, he walked to where Gerd was pinned, gripped the spear, and pulled it away.

Gerd stood. His throat healed.

"Still a god," Atticus said, watching the wound close.

"But not for long."

"You're still a bastard."

"The worst," Gerd agreed.

"She'll hate you."

"Probably. But for once, this isn't about me."

Atticus looked at Gerd for a very long time. Then he corrected his opposite: *"Us."*

Gerd looked down at the thousands of scattered Unwanted: all his life's worst memories finally out in the open. But for the first time ever, he was finally willing to look them all in the eye.

"It might not make any difference," Atticus said, knowing without words what Gerd was thinking.

"Maybe not, but look at it this way …"

Atticus, for the first time since Gerd had met him, smiled. And then he finished Gerd's thought. "We can't possibly make it any worse."

They took each other's hands.

Ran.

And jumped headlong into the pit, tumbling down and down and down.

Chapter Twenty-Four

X-RAYS, MRIs, CAT scans, blood tests.

They had to rule out physical abnormalities first, but Lucas knew everything would come up negative. He didn't have cancer or parasites or a concussion that had somehow been forgotten. He knew what had triggered that final episode (Shelby walking in on him and Miranda, saying such unlovely things), but more importantly *he knew it was an episode*.

Didn't make it any easier, though. You might be able to cure a tumor, but it was a lot harder to run from your own mind.

Miranda had driven him to the emergency room after he'd spied Shelby, passed out, then hit his head. But she had no way of knowing that he clearly remembered — in a supernaturally tactile dream — being shot, stabbed, beaten, vivisected, nearly decapitated, and run through with a spear. He didn't want to breathe a word about it. The visions had the force of memories, enough that he was having trouble swallowing — and if the ER told him he still had a piece of pole in his throat, he really would go insane.

Miranda wanted to hold him, but he told her to go home and rest. She wanted to make him feel better because for the first time in anyone's memory, the unassailable Lucas Latham was frightened right out of his mind.

But he didn't want comfort. The person in life who'd been best to him was a victim of his betrayal, and the person who still loved him unconditionally he'd no doubt ruined for life. Accepting Miranda's soothing words felt like yet another betrayal: this time, of life itself. Taking any comfort was like giving all good things the bird. He was a son of a bitch … and finally, undeniably, he'd come to face it as a fact.

The night was long and he spent it intentionally alone. By the time the ER cleared him it was nearly two in the morning. He called a FASTr to take him home. The driver's name was Cole and he wore a Rastafarian hat big enough to block the rearview.

"Where you goin' tonight, my friend?"

"Home." Instead of *to Hell.*

He didn't sleep. He paced. And paced. And paced. Everything was new. There was so much about the house he'd been blind to. So much he hadn't allowed himself to see. Until Miranda the other night — and then Shelby to follow — he hadn't even remembered the snow globe.

Why would he? If he saw the globe, he'd have to remember his wedding photos too, still displayed atop a hutch. He'd have to acknowledge the stain in the garage where Kate's car had leaked oil. He'd have to notice her hair, rolled into big blonde dust bunnies in the closets. He'd have to see her favorite music stacked next to the speakers. He'd have to notice the phone number sheet, for school, tacked to the fridge and written in Kate's familiar script.

Everything looked, sounded, and smelled of her. Everything looked, sounded, and smelled like self-made sorrow.

The last thing he noticed, in the medicine cabinet, was the Klonopin refill that Kate hadn't touched. It was a controlled substance; no doctor would prescribe the pills twice. A nearly full vial still in the cabinet after her suicide meant she'd been squirreling pills. Getting refills on the same schedule despite not needing them. She had stockpiled through months of neglect. All that planning. Lucas wondered how long that had gone on for. In their last days, how many moments had they shared in which she'd already been half-dead? How many small ways had she begged for a line to cling to ... and yet he had given her nothing?

You're ignorant and a bastard, Lucas tried to tell himself, *but that doesn't make you evil.*

And another voice inside said, *Yeah, yeah.*

Lucas got the vodka from the freezer.

He sat on the couch.

And with the vial clasped sweaty in his right hand, he waited.

And wondered.

And waited.

He lapsed in and out of sleep. Between nods, he revisited the island prison, suddenly able to see every bit of it.

This is how people must feel after amnesia ends.

But no, that wasn't right. So he corrected his thought.

This is how people feel when they recall repressed trauma.

The trauma that had been buried inside him, layers deep, guarded by gatekeepers in the depths of his mind — all of it was in the open now. But should he feel sorry for himself? No. Down that path lay delusion.

Miranda called in the morning. She told him she

hoped he was okay, which he somehow was despite the vodka, the pills, and a half-baked idea to use them. She was kind to him, and her kindness felt like a cruelty. She said she was sorry, of all things. She said she hadn't meant to shock him into … into some kind of an *episode*.

He started to explain and she told him it would all be fine. He shouldn't blame himself. He looked at the pills and vodka still on the coffee table and told her the truth: *I do. And I always will.*

But he couldn't die. Right now, that was the most selfish thing he could do.

Therapy.

Therapy.

And more therapy.

Lucas almost wanted to be diagnosed with a big-ticket disorder — something that tossed a person irreparably into the looney bin.

Mr. Latham, your brain is broken. Mr. Latham, you've fallen apart like Humpty Dumpty, but there's a problem: even if all of Gerd's horses and all Atticus's men could put you back together again, they'd refuse because let's be honest, you should die in a fire.

But the physical tests came back negative and the psychological tests cast him as a narcissist.

Clinical narcissism? he'd asked. Emphasis on *clinical*. Clinical things were afflictions a person couldn't help. But the shrink just looked him in the eye, having already heard the vomited version of his story, and Lucas could read his message as clearly as if it were a diagnosis in itself.

No, sir. Turns out, you're just an asshole.

He put on a good face for Shelby. Sent her to a well-reviewed child psychologist, and joined her when he was requested and permitted, half-wanting to offer all his worldly belongings to the doctor in penance.

Finally someone — a nurse with no business butting in

— grabbed him by the shoulder on his way from one appointment to another. "You're here a lot. A lot lot lot."

Lucas started to recite his story. It was a reflex now, like throwing up.

"Not my business, I guess," said the nurse, stopping Lucas before he started back in on the story they'd all heard plenty of times before, "but if you wanna help that girl of yours, there's something you need to know."

"What?"

He leaned in, so nobody would overhear. "There's a difference between confession and whining." Then the nurse nearly poked Lucas in his chest. "Maybe this was about your little girl at the start. But now?" He shook his head. "Now, it's about you."

"I screwed her up. I—"

"I know what you did. But are you gonna keep apologizing for the dad you were … or are you gonna do the hard thing, step up, carry your guilt … and start being the father she needs?"

To that, Lucas had no reply.

Chapter Twenty-Five

THE ISLAND on which they took their vacation felt lost in time.

Getting there meant either a ferry or a terrifying little plane ride. The roads were all dirt and there was no grocery store — just a co-op and some enterprising resident's back porch, which was unmarked and functioned as an honor-system convenience store with a chained-down cash box.

The island itself was north, in the middle of a giant lake: freshwater, not salt.

At first Lucas hadn't wanted to go. Islands were sort of a trigger for him now. At first he came solely on Miranda's invite; her parents had a cottage there. She told him to get over himself. Their affair was barely an affair: it was sex, once, and afterward the sad fact of Kate's death had shoved them together. They weren't dating or anything beyond it, so nothing they did now could be inappropriate.

Lucas had lied to her back then and lied to them both afterward, but for some reason she'd forgiven him. Theirs was not a love story. It probably wouldn't have a happy ending. He hadn't neglected the wife to earn the girlfriend, but somehow he'd managed to keep her as a friend. He tried to say she couldn't and shouldn't forgive him, but that bit of self-indulgent tripe turned her serious.

I think I'll decide for myself what I do, she told him, and after that he'd let it be.

He was on an elevated section of deck, looking out at the water, when Miranda pulled up alongside and handed him a beer.

"Stop," she said.

"What?"

"Whatever this is."

"I'm just standing here."

"You're a shit, Lucas. You just can't figure it out."

He turned, hip to the railing, and looked at her incredulously.

"First you're like a goddamn dictator. And now you're a martyr. You know why nobody likes martyrs?"

"People like martyrs," Lucas said.

"Because with martyrs, it's all about them."

"You think I'm making this all about me."

She sipped her beer. "You did for a long time."

"But not anymore."

"Not as much. I know you want to make sure nobody thinks you're rebounding with me, but we're not together. And besides."

"Besides?"

"Besides, who gives a shit what people think?"

Lucas narrowed his eyes. "Who are you?"

"Not someone you're going to fool, that's for sure. Not some chica you'll bed by lying."

"So it's just lying that's off-limits."

She rolled her eyes. "Buy me dinner first."

They watched the waves.

"I wasn't pining out here," Lucas told her. "Or trying to look all forlorn so you would come out and talk to me."

"Sure."

"I'm serious."

"Sure you are."

Lucas laughed, then sat. The sky was blue and the day warm. "I can't get it out of my head, Miranda. I keep trying, but it just won't go."

"Kate?"

That hurt. But it was his job, now, to accept that hurt. He'd be paying for Kate for the rest of his life, and he'd have to do it without notice, without soliciting pity, without complaint. It was his duty to hurt in silence. It was the one way, even with help, that he'd be forever alone.

"Of course Kate. But I mean the …"

When the pause went too long, Miranda followed his eyes across the water, along the rocky beach.

"The island," she said. He'd finally told her everything. Every bit of his delusion.

Lucas nodded. "I don't know if coming here was a good idea or a bad idea."

"Good. Not bad. For both of you."

She might have said *both* pointedly or just because it made sense. Either way, it turned Lucas's mind back to where it belonged: not to himself, but to Shelby. She was what mattered most. His *Shel* — his little *Sea Shell,* as Kate had dubbed her on their Hawaii vacation.

"You sound so sure," Lucas said.

"Because I am, dumbass. You weren't on an island. You were … inside your head or something. People break down. It happens. What matters is what you do after."

"You take a self-help course or something?"

She sipped again without looking at him. "Let's just say I had my own island."

"Not literally," Lucas said.

"No. Not literally. But … Tell you a secret?"

"Always."

"What I just told you … it's the same thing I keep telling myself."

Lucas exhaled. Shook his head. "It was so real. Sometimes I wonder if it was. Is that crazy?"

"Yes."

"I've analyzed it using all sorts of dream books. I watched a bunch of weird movies, wondering if I would see any similar messages." He pointed the butt of his bottle at her. "You know the one thing that comes back more than anything else? It's weird. Totally by-the-way. Just something I heard once, and at the time it wasn't at all a big deal."

"What was that?"

"Something the guy in the pit said."

"The guy made of bugs."

"Right. I … well, I guess it was Gerd, the guy I was there; you know … I asked the Gatekeeper once if I was being taken to something new. And, you know, things like that in dreams or whatever, they sort of talk in circles. Answer questions with questions. Stuff like that."

"Fuckin' demons," Miranda said.

"But when I asked about 'something new,' you know what the bug-thing said?"

Miranda waited.

"It said, 'Only one thing is ever truly new.'"

"*What* one thing?"

"That's just it." He shrugged. "I don't know."

"Hmm. Did you ask your guy about it?"

Lucas barely heard her. His eyes had strayed lazily to the beach, where neighbors strolled by in the tiny lapping waves. Nonchalant and seemingly unseen, was a shark the size of a semi.

The shark lolled in the shallow, mouth open, its tiny black eyes trained on Lucas. Even across the distance it seemed to say, *Where you go, I go.*

"Lucas?"

He turned back to Miranda.

"I said, 'Did you ask your guy about it?' About the 'one thing is new'?"

"He said it came from my head. It must have been something I thought I needed to know."

"So he was no help."

Lucas shrugged.

"Fuckin' doctors," Miranda said after another long sip. "They're worse than demons."

THE NICE THING about the island was all the nothing to do. There was no internet, and the only TV was over-air … and with sketchy reception. Their options were to read, play games, read, talk, read, sleep, or maybe take a walk. They'd even started a puzzle — something Lucas hadn't done since childhood.

By that second afternoon, he was pleasantly bored. The trip — five days in total — was already doing its job of forcibly clearing his mind. *Getting away from it all* was a real thing.

So he rallied Shelby, who'd already read and puzzled her fill, then they borrowed the Millners' car and drove from one end of the tiny island to the other. He found the western shore next, just to reassure himself that the island had one. Most of the interior acreage was farmland and vineyards. They saw very few people.

They got out at the south end and walked down a very long, sandy point. It was like a large sandbar, and took nearly a half hour to walk in just one direction. When they came back, they sat at a picnic table and listened to the screech of gulls.

"I miss Mommy," Shelby said.

Another dagger pierced his heart. Lucas found himself wanting to fall on a sword for this story, but Shelby already knew far more than any seven-year-old should. He'd done all his confession, and somehow she still loved him anyway.

So he simply put his arm around her and said, "I do too, kid."

"She was sick."

"Yeah."

"Daddy?"

"Yeah."

"You wanna hear something?"

"Sure."

"I think …" Shelby stalled, practically choking on a thought that was clearly too big for her. Lucas turned a little, giving her the rest of his attention. This was serious, whatever it was. "I just … I think she'd forgive you."

"I don't know, Shel. I try to be better now, but I wasn't then."

"Yeah. I know. But. You know."

It wasn't really an explanation. But for Shelby, in this situation, it also sort of was. He hugged her closer to him.

"I know 'cause of what she said when Stacy broke my Etch A Sketch."

Lucas felt himself frown. He remembered that. It had happened not far from the end, when he'd been his worst and Kate had too. Shelby had found some videos online, then went about creating a downright prodigious bit of art on that rather ordinary toy. She'd set it on her desk, propped up like a painting. Until a visiting girl, Stacy Cray, had knocked it over in an argument. Then stomped on it. Broken the art ahead of its canvas. Afterward, the girl had been inconsolable. Long after Shelby said it was okay, Stacy kept on apologizing.

"What did Mom say?" Lucas asked.

"She said that every mistake is a chance for a new start. You mess up, and it's like shaking the Etch A Sketch. You get to do it all over."

Lucas hugged her again.

Then a gull screeched overhead, nearly close enough to hit them. He ducked, half-swore, and watched the bird as it circled to land on a post in the water.

Which was part of a dock hidden by cattails — a dock he hadn't seen.

He stood.

"Look, Daddy! It's a dock! Maybe we can go fishing!"

Shelby ran for it, but Lucas ran slower. Because he could see the dock now, and it rang an old bell deep inside his mind. The thing appeared to be floating, not anchored. It was long and unwieldy, wagging into the water like the island's tail.

"Shelby …"

But she was on it in a second, at the end, fussing with something.

"Shelby!"

"Look, Daddy! There's a rope!"

He walked forward. Stepped on the wood. The thing gave but did not sink. It was stable enough, just ugly. And Shelby was right; there was a rope tied off at the end. It hung right into the water.

Shelby was already on her knees. She pulled. Rope coiled on the dock behind her.

"Honey. Leave that alone."

But she was looking down, watching the depths. She

saw something and choked up on the rope, moving to her knees to fetch it.

"Shelby! That's someone's—!"

But he'd arrived by now, and he saw exactly what was at the rope's end.

"It's a lobster trap, Daddy!"

He shook his head. "Lobsters live in saltwater."

"But look!"

"SHELBY, DAMMIT, LISTEN TO ME AND DON'T TOUCH THAT!"

The girl recoiled, a little hurt, but she'd already recovered the trap from the water.

Lucas approached, gun shy. Shelby had indeed found a lobster trap. In freshwater. There was no lobster inside, but there was something between its wooden slats.

The girl set the trap on the deck, reached inside, and came out with a single, smooth black stone.

But then it collapsed in her hands, and Lucas saw that the stone was only clay; his eyes had been playing tricks on him.

He exhaled relief. "Put it back. It's not ours. You need to listen out here, okay? This dock is old. Could be dangerous."

"I'm sorry, Daddy."

"It's okay. But let's not pull on all the lines we see in the water, okay?"

Shelby nodded.

Back at the car, Lucas looked toward the dock and realized he could no longer see it. Maybe it had never even been there.

They got into the car and closed the doors. Lucas looked at the dock's location for a few long seconds, then returned his attention to Shelby.

"I'm sorry I yelled out there."

She surprised him by smiling.

"What?" he said.

"Something new," she said.

"What?"

"That's what I was going to tell you. About what Mommy said. About Stacy and the Etch A Sketch?"

He shook his head, not understanding.

"Forgiveness," Shelby explained.

"I don't follow."

"Forgiveness," she repeated. "Mommy used to say that most people just repeat themselves over and over … but forgiveness is the only thing that's really new."

Lucas moved his eyes from the reeds, where the dock lay, to the lake's blue expanse beyond. He imagined himself spying the future out there, no longer looking to the past.

There were no fins in the water. No sharks. No sharp white teeth among the swells.

"Let's head back and go swimming," he said to Shelby. "It's a beautiful day."

This where I suggest the book you should read next to spare you hours of searching, right? Cool. I can do that.

All of my MANY books (and their suggested reading order) are at JohnnyBTruantBooks.com, but personally I'd suggest:

THE TARGET: A mindfuck of a thriller with eight assassins, one high-profile target … and a story that's not what you think.

Brothers Emil and Robert are assassins seeking one last hit before they get out of the game. So when a bounty goes out on Senator Simon Bisset, it seems a payday worth chasing. Just one problem: The bounty's an open call — and unlike Emil, the competition isn't falling to pieces.

Get *The Target* cheaper at JohnnyBTruantBooks.com

Enter the Truantverse

When it comes to stories and the worlds they live in, books are only the beginning.

Visit JohnnyBTruant.com/join to get my best books sooner and cheaper than the other stores.

My list doesn't suck like so many author email lists. Seriously. It has unicorns.

Also by Johnny B. Truant

Winter Break

Pattern Black

Pretty Killer

Cursed

The Bialy Pimps

Namaste

The Target

La Fleur de Blanc

Axis of Aaron

Devil May Care

Screenplay

The Island

Burnout

Sick and Wired

UNICORN WESTERN:

Unicorn Western

The Wanderers

A Fistful of Magic

Shimmer to Yuma

The Man Who Shot Alan Whitney

The Spectacular Seven

Open Meadows

The Unforgotten

The Magic Bunch

Unicorn Genesis

~

FAT VAMPIRE:

Fat Vampire

Fat Vampire 2: Tastes Like Chicken

Fat Vampire 3: All You Can Eat

Fat Vampire 4: Harder Better Fatter Stronger

Fat Vampire 5: Fatpocalypse

Fat Vampire 6: Survival of the Fattest

The Vampire Maurice

Anarchy and Blood

Vampires in the White City

Fangs and Fame

Game of Fangs

~

INVASION:

Invasion

Contact

Colonization

Annihilation

Judgment

Extinction

Resurrection

Save the City

Save the Girl

Save the World

Longshot

THE INEVITABLE:

Robot Proletariat

The Infinite Loop

The Hard Reset

Cascade Failure

Reboot

En3my

DEAD CITY:

Dead City

Dead Nation

Dead Planet

Dead Zero

Empty Nest

THE DREAM ENGINE:

The Dream Engine

The Nightmare Factory

The Ruby Room

The Pandora Core

The Engine Convergence

The Tinkerer's Mainspring

~

GORE POINT:

Gore Point 1

Gore Point 2

Gore Point 3

~

THE BEAM:

The Beam: Season One

The Beam: Season Two

The Beam: Season Three

The Beam Season Four

The Beam Season Five

Future Proof

Plugged

The Future of Sex

~

THE TOMORROW GENE:

The Tomorrow Gene

The Eden Experiment

The Tomorrow Clone

Null Identity

~

COMEDIES:

Everyone Gets Divorced

Greens

Fiends

Decoy Wallet

NONFICTION:

The Fiction Formula

Fiction Unboxed

Iterate & Optimize

The Story Solution

Write. Publish. Repeat.

The One With All the Writing Advice